The Cat at Mrs. Drimley's Door

By Anna E. Turner

The Cat at Mrs. Drimley's Door
Published by Enchantment Press
Hessel, Michigan 49745

DISCLAIMER: This is a work of fiction. Any resemblance to actual persons, places, cats, or events is coincidental.

ISBN: 978-0-9979511-9-6

Prologue

Florie lowered the flame under the whistling kettle, poured the piping hot water into a porcelain teapot so crackled with age the tea threatened to burst onto the cloth below it, then turned to level an appraising glance on her company.

"Please, Florie, say you'll help. There must be something you can do."

"Of course there is, but it won't come without cost. You'll be off free. Tell me, why would you have others pay the price of your freedom?" Florie stared directly into his eyes as she dropped a stringing dollop of honey into his teacup without asking whether he'd like some or not.

He didn't reply. He just gazed, entranced by the steam rising artfully from the hot mug as she poured the tea.

Whatever his thoughts, she would not hear them, but she knew that before she'd needled him with the truth. He was, by nature, infuriatingly close lipped.

His voice was nearly wistful when he finally spoke, "So, can I count on you?"

Florie gave a sharp nod, full of disgust. Though her eyes clouded over with disapproval, the gesture could not wash away the affection flowing rampantly between the companions. She'd been wrong in her assessment of him, this much was becoming obvious with a suddenness that perturbed her. She'd been preparing the wrong person for the job, and she was not used to being wrong.

Florie watched as her guest gripped his still hot mug, downed the contents through his bearded lips, and swallowed hard in a single scalding gulp that made Florie's throat shudder. As he stood to leave, she impulsively gripped his sleeve, invading his gaze with her unwavering glare.

"I'll miss you."

"Aye. And I you, old friend." And with the subtlest glimmer in his usually lively eyes, he was gone.

Florie shut the door softly and returned to her tea. It had cooled, so she passed her veiny hand over its top, then took a perfectly warmed sip. She sipped quietly, waiting for Edgar to descend the stairs. It was likely he had overheard. He was probably already getting ready. It was a part of his

gift, after all. He'd been with the family for ages, assisting in times like these. And something must be done now. She would need help, no doubt about it. But Florie did not like the foreboding mood that had been left behind by her guest. Something was different this time around. Edgar must be feeling it, too. Why else would he still be hiding away upstairs?

"Edgar, come down please. There's no use beating about the bush."

Edgar slunk down the stairs. "I don't necessarily have a good feeling about this, but it's been coming on for some time. There's been a good spread between requests, hasn't there?"

"Yes," Florie replied sadly.

"That horrible, hacking man!" Edgar stated with contempt. "I knew he wasn't the one."

"Yes, you were right all along," Florie replied absently.

Florie and Edgar stayed up late into the night considering ideas. A plan was made, loosely, as always, for there was little that could be done to direct the progress once it had begun. All they could do was be willing, make a decent plan, and get on with it—trusting that the strong intentions would bear out in the end.

For Edgar's gift to work, he had to completely surrender to it, allow himself to be swallowed up whole by the needs of another. He never knew where or in what form he'd find himself, or where his work would take him. In fact,

upon awakening, he forgot his true identity. This was a necessary part of his work. After he awoke it was all instinct, faith, and pure, selfless courage. Once his assignment was fulfilled, Edgar was released from his contract and freed back into his natural form.

This is all to say that Edgar went to great lengths to be of assistance. He'd done it hundreds of times, so there was no good reason to feel afraid this time. He agreed without fanfare. Colorful as he was, Edgar always took his assignments seriously. It was, after all, his sole purpose.

Florie made all the necessary arrangements while Edgar prepared himself for initiation. As he prepared, deep in his heart, Edgar knew he'd never be the same again. He never really was after an assignment. It made him melancholy to think of yet another transformation. Even so, his commitment to duty called him onward.

"Well, old chap," Edgar said to himself in the mirror, "here's to another adventure."

Florie appeared at the door with a handkerchief—she always got emotional on initiation days. It got so quiet in the house without Edgar around, but this was her work, too. Keen observation. Stealthy guidance. Oversight and management. These were her roles.

"Steady on, Florie," Edgar crooned.

"Yes, Yes. Are you ready?" Florie asked as she unfolded the contract she held in her hands, which promptly glowed golden and sputtered up a yellow flame.

"As I'll ever be," Edgar replied, and with a wink he reached out. At the slightest touch, Edgar, the flame, and the contract disappeared.

Part One

How It Began

Mulligan

Mrs. Elsa Dora Drimley lived in a tall and crooked house at the edge of a tall and crooked cliff along an inlet on a northern shore. Her cat, Mulligan, was quite bitter about his name. Who would want to be named after stew? Mrs. Drimley was a practical sort of woman, though, and had served her husband one variation or another of stew, which Mr. Drimley affectionately referred to as his helping of mulligan, each and every night of their twenty-seven years together.

You don't know what mulligan is? Well, neither did I, which means that we are fortunate folks, indeed. Mulligan is stew made of whatever you have on hand. You just throw it in the pot and stuff it in the oven or boil it on the stove (or over a fire if it's what you've got) and call it dinner. Mr. Drimley knew of mulligan from his days traveling the rails as a hobo.

When he was only ten, he had struck out on his own. He had spent enough time begging on the street for his father. He was getting too old for pity now, and he was tired of his father's rough hands leaving fresh bruises. How he'd survived on his own, he'd never been able to explain. He had always had a lucky streak even as a boy. Something in him had told him, *go*, and he'd gone, leaving his father passed out on the hard ground. The gypsy lady with the eyes that saw down to your soul, the one who had insisted he learn to read, had stepped into the alley as he slid through the night. Without a word, she'd thrust a bundle of food scraps tied into a handkerchief into his hands, then disappeared back into the shadows. He'd lived off the scraps, wondering how there seemed to always be just enough for one more meal. It lasted until the day he came upon a hobo camp.

After that, he made his way working from town to town, camping and traveling with the hobos who taught him how to build, how to carve, how to take pride in work. Then, years later, he heard the voice again. *Go.* He knew where he was going: away from the trains and the cities, up north to the still wild place—to freedom and adventure. He walked for what felt like eons without seeing anything but trees and the creatures that live in and among them. He walked until he saw water so vast he thought it was the ocean, and there he stayed, as there was nowhere further north to go.

At first he thought he was alone in that place, but of course there were others. The longer he stayed, the more people there were, but by that time, he'd built his home on the cliff by the water. He was there to stay. So, when a settlement began to build up on the other side of the peninsula, he used it to his benefit. Mr. Drimley began selling fish.

By the time he had married Mrs. Drimley, Mr. Drimley had a rhythm to his days. He would climb down the cliff every day, take his hand-made, ramshackle boat out to sea and gather fish in a net on the way to the port market. There, he would sell them all away, save ten heads, per Mrs. Drimley's request. He kept the heads wrapped in brown waxy paper in a backpack basket, which had been woven from willow branches by Mrs. Drimley, to be carried up the cliff to the Drimley's ramshackle home. Mrs. Drimley would drop the fish heads one at a time into her pot of simmering herbs and wild greens and root vegetables. When the day was getting long and dark, she'd fish the bones out of the pot. What was left in the pot was their dinner.

When he was forty five, Mr. Drimley became ill with a cough that would not leave. All the herbs in the forest would not make the cough go away, though Mrs. Drimley prepared them in every way she knew of: a balm for his chest, a potion to be swallowed, a tub of tea to soak in. The cough would not be treated.

A week before Mr. Drimley died, when Mrs. Drimley was nearly to the point of despair, she opened her door to find a tiny grey fluff of a kitten with violet eyes sitting next to three fish. Mrs. Drimley was bewildered by this kitten that was able to catch and carry fish twice as large as himself up the crooked cliff, but she would not welcome a cat into the house. Every day for the next week, the kitten appeared with an offering of three fish, with which Mrs. Drimley would make her stew. The stew was much improved by the use of whole fish rather than just the heads. The innards of these three fish became the cat's dinner. On the morning of the day Mr. Drimley died, Mrs. Drimley brought the cat inside with her and made him a bargain. She would shelter him if he would promise to become as domesticated as possible and if he would continue to bring her three fish every day. She felt it fitting to call him Mulligan.

Mulligan immediately argued that his name should not refer to the horrid stew she was incessantly boiling on the stove. He demanded that he be called something regal, like Charles, but in the early days, Mrs. Drimley did not quite know how to understand Mulligan. And so it was that Mulligan began his extraordinary life with Mrs. Drimley. Had he been any other cat at any other door, his life might have been perfectly ordinary. But it was not to be.

An Unusual Kittenhood

Mrs. Drimley set out domesticating Mulligan right away. The first lesson was that Mulligan should not bring any offerings to the door of the house except for the three fish each day. Mice hunting in the house was encouraged. However, the mice should be properly and thoroughly disposed of in the way of cats. Never on the kitchen rug, of course. And never should any evidence of the ordeal be left lying around to be found. Mulligan learned this lesson most unpleasantly through shrieks of disgust and harsh reprimands coming from Mrs. Drimley when she stumbled upon a trio of mouse corpses on the back stoop, and again when she found nothing but a tiny paw and a skinny grey tail near the hearth. Soon enough Mulligan followed these rules without fail.

The second lesson was that Mulligan was never to sit directly on the furniture. Mrs. Drimley found it much more pleasing to see a cat on a cushion. Mulligan believed this to be exceptionally ridiculous, but being a

cat who understood the importance of aesthetics, he begrudgingly agreed to this rule so long as the cushion was freshly plumped and cleared of any evidence of yesterday's shedding each morning. Mrs. Drimley was, understandably, a poor housekeeper during this time of bereavement.

Mulligan patiently waited beside the cushion each morning after his trip behind the outhouse for Mrs. Drimley to do her plumping and clearing. He was not above making a terrible racket of moaning to get her attention if she was too occupied with her knitting to notice the kitten whose haunches were growing increasingly chilled on the wooden floor. Mulligan thought Mrs. Drimley's floors could stand a braided rug, but she was grieving, poor woman, and he was sensitive to her need for rest during this difficult time. When she was beyond her grief, he would insist that this floor get a rug.

These two rules got the housemates by well enough. Mrs. Drimley was too exhausted by her grief to demand much more of the kitten, and so many months passed. The rest of Mulligan's tiniest kittenhood, as a matter of fact, was spent with one lady knitting wool in her chair, one kitten growing ever so steadily into a cat, perching on a cushion on the stiff sofa, and one empty chair in a rug-less living room. Each day, mid-morning, the kitten would sneak quietly out to fetch the fish before returning to his cushion. Each day, after the cat returned, the lady would

fetch her herbs, clean the fish and pile all into a pot that would simmer all day on the stove.

A kittenhood spent quietly sitting is unusual, and it is an unusual kitten who is able to do it. Mulligan was an old soul, this much is clear. All of that sitting and quiet left a great deal of time for thinking. When one is still on the outside, it often happens that one is active on the inside. Such was the case with Mulligan. Mulligan created a whole world of ideas in his head as he watched Mrs. Drimley knit sock after shawl after mitten. Mulligan also watched the sizable yarn basket. Soon it would be empty. And then what would happen?

Unlike Mulligan, Mrs. Drimley was not thinking. Mrs. Drimley was stitching her broken heart. If not for the stitching there would have been weeping. She knew this, because when the stitching and the stewing and the scrubbing of the pot were done for the day, her pillow collected silent tears. Silent. Because if there was no one lying on the other pillow to hear the sobs, why let them be loud? Had there been a soul to hear them, would she have let them hear? I don't know. She had never done before.

She could not be grateful for the kitten who brought her fish. She could scarcely feel at all. But if not for the kitten on the cushion on the davenport, the empty chair beside her would have been unbearable. And if not for the offering of fish she would have forgotten to eat day

after day. So Mulligan was saving Mrs. Drimley. But that was to be understood much later.

As Mrs. Drimley drew a fresh ball of yarn from her basket, she did not see that her supply was getting low. She just knit and knit and knit to the beat of her aching heart.

An Alarmingly Brief History
of Elsa Dora Drimley

Before we move on with our story, we must learn a few things about our Elsa Dora Drimley, and how she came to live in the tall crooked house beside the tall crooked cliff. Imagine Elsa Dora. She is fourteen years old. Her hair is still bright and golden, but her blue eyes are already clouded grey. She has a dingey white hat. She stands in the snow with thin, filthy shoes on her feet. She is wrapped in layers of shawls with holes over a drab dress. She carries firewood. Do you see her? Wait until you see her.

Good.

She lives deep in the woods. No vast body of water to be seen or even heard of. She is the last of many children. Her mother is dead. She carries the firewood. She boils the water. She strips the beds. She airs the house. She never learned to read. Nor did she ever learn to long for anything. She answers the shrill calls of her siblings all day and dusts around her poor broken-hearted father who can't move

from his chair. Life swirls loudly around her, and Elsa Dora carries firewood. Boils water. Strips beds. Airs the house.

Then one day when she was fourteen, gathering firewood in the forest, a tune catches her ear. She's never heard anything like it. She doesn't even know the word jolly. She stops and listens as the sound moves closer. Then she is face to face with a lad whose cheeks were as red as his ruddy hair.

"Hello," he says before continuing his tune.

Elsa Dora stares stupidly at this odd creature who grins wildly at her in return.

"I say. Hello!" he repeats.

"Hello," Elsa Dora barely whispers. And this one hello changes the course of Elsa Dora's life, for the ruddy haired and red-cheeked lad was none other than Mr. Drimley who four years later led Elsa Dora through the woods to the sea. There he taught her to read and brought her beautiful things to fill the crooked house by the crooked cliff. The fateful error in all of this was that Mr. Drimley, who had never craved calm when life whirl chaotically around him, loved adventure. And in teaching Elsa Dora to be free he found a grand adventure. He did not realize, though, that not all free people love adventure. And so, when his Mrs. Drimley, all set free, was at ease and contentment with their steady life by the sea, he grew more and more restless. The quiet drew him to the cough, which drew him to his death. For as much as he wished it, love for another can't change a soul. And his soul had to *go.*

This is the alarmingly short history of Elsa Dora Drimley. But it requires no more than this. Elsa Dora had chaos without longing and then she had calm without longing, which she much preferred. The constants were carrying the firewood. Boiling the water. Stripping the bed. Airing the house. And she found comfort in them.

Something quite odd and decidedly unfair to the love of Elsa Dora Drimley and her Mr. Drimley happened once he had breathed his last. Maybe it was from eating whole fish in her stew instead of heads. Or maybe it was the absolute silence that Mrs. Drimley had never known at such lengths. Maybe it was the cat.

In future years, Mrs. Drimley spent many fire lit hours wondering just what had tipped the balance. Whatever caused it, Elsa Dora Drimley began to long. Of course, she did not know the sensation, and so she did not recognize it for longing. Therefore, it only added to the ache in her heart. Ever so slowly, she ceased to stitch grief and began to stitch longing. The transformation of stitching was so subtle that she never knew it happened. But Mulligan felt it, and he watched Mrs. Drimley closely. Oh yes, something had changed. And it was about to change everything.

The Knitting Basket Poses a Dilemma

One day, I believe it was a Tuesday, once the fish had been offered, the stew put to the pot, Mrs. Drimley put to her seat, and Mulligan to his cushion, Mrs. Drimley reached into her knitting basket and retrieved the last ball of yarn. Mulligan watched with wonder. Would she notice? No, she would not.

Mulligan had caught on to Mrs. Drimley's reliance on her daily sameness. He began to have a small panic inside, for he'd learned to love this simple lady, and what would become of her if her yarn ran out? What would she do? Of course, Mulligan hadn't known a time when Mrs. Drimley carried the wood, boiled the water, stripped the beds, and aired the house. All that ended the day her husband died. Which was, as you'll remember, the day Mulligan was invited inside. Really, the house could have done with a very thorough airing, as it had been months and months. Not to mention, winter was coming and no wood had been gathered at all. Mulligan

only knew that Mrs. Drimley must knit and knit and knit.

He shifted on his cushion.

As the end of the yarn began to dance in the basket, and then sidle up toward Mrs. Drimley's stitching hands, Mulligan's heart pounded. He quietly climbed off of the cushion and glided beside the sofa. Mrs. Drimley gave no sign of noticing his movement. Mulligan crouched as he crawled across the bare floor toward the yarn basket between the empty chair and Mrs. Drimley's. And then he crept inside. He batted at the dangling yarn once, twice, and then it was gone, slipping over the arm of the chair. Mrs. Drimley could see the tail of the yarn moving closer to her knitting fingers. She absently reached down toward the basket beside her chair, then drew suddenly back when she felt fur instead of yarn. She slowly peered over the arm of the chair and saw Mulligan sitting in the basket looking right up at her. She watched as he raised his paw toward her, then let it drift slowly down. Tentatively, Mulligan perched his furry front paws on the side of the chair, and with his violet eyes peered intently at Mrs. Drimley.

He'd never had such a good look at her face. Her blond hair, growing ashen with age and badly in need of washing, was pulled haphazardly back in a bun at the nape of her neck. Her skin was deathly pale and it sagged over the drawn-in pockets of her cheeks. Her lips flaked in front of crooked teeth that had been well cared for before her husband's death, but now were threatening decay

if not seen to at once. Mulligan stared deeply into Mrs. Drimley's eyes, blue as a stormy summer sky, but flat and expressionless. They began to gloss over when suddenly, Mulligan felt a drip on his nose, then another on his fur. He looked toward the ceiling in alarm, but it was only Mrs. Drimley raining tears on his furry head.

Mrs. Drimley slumped over in her chair, and moments later her shoulders began to shudder. Huge gulping sobs escaped her, and it seemed to Mulligan each one said, "At last. At last," as they made their way into the world. One arm dangled over the side of the chair. The other lay limply in her lap. The woman only moved to shake the sorrow drenched wails from her torso. Mulligan determinedly walked around the chair and leapt right into Mrs. Drimley's lap where he curled up and made himself completely still until her sobbing ceased.

As Mrs. Drimley became still, Mulligan watched her piercingly while his head still laid on her lap. When the time was right, I don't know how he knew, Mulligan rose up on his haunches and placed his front paws below Mrs. Drimley's face on the faded floral arm of the chair.

Then, by sheer force of will, Mulligan said, "My dear Mrs. Drimley. There is wood to be carried, and work to be done. If we are to survive, we must go on living."

And remarkably, Mrs. Drimley understood every word.

Part Two

How It Continues

Mrs. Drimley Goes on Living

Catching fish was much trickier in the winter. Still, Mulligan faithfully brought three fish to the door, returning half frozen and covered with snowflakes. Mulligan sat by the hearth for one full hour as he unthawed. First tiny icicles would melt and drip from the tips of his lengthy whiskers with a sizzle on the grey hearthstone. Then his fur would grow heavily damp as the snow drops turned to water drops which soaked him to the skin. When he could finally feel his paws again, he'd shakily lift them to begin grooming himself back to warmth. Once he was dried out to his usual ashy grey, he'd assume his place on the cushion on the davenport for a much deserved nap. For that much had not changed. But nearly everything else had.

You see, Mrs. Drimley had woken from her slumber,

so to speak. That is to say, she began to live again. In the last moments of autumn, Mrs. Drimley had wandered the woods gathering all the loose branches and twigs she could find. It was not a lot, but it would do if she were careful to use just enough every day. She also dug up all the roots from the garden and packed them into the cellar. Wonders. The boughs had gone on falling for her. The roots she'd planted so long ago had grown strong and plentiful with no help at all, even in the absolute mess that had descended on and in the garden soil.

Once a meager survival was assured, and winter chased her indoors, Mrs. Drimley became truly aware of her surroundings for the first time since her husband's death. For a moment she just sat, looking around dumbfounded. For during those months while she'd been stitching her sorrow away the dust had not ceased to fall onto the mantle and floor. Where had it come from, she wondered, with noone to move about in the house but herself, as ghostlike as she had been. There was a grimy film in the kitchen that used to gleam and glisten from her routine scrubbing. The bed covers were appalling. The air was dank.

Mrs. Drimley put water on to boil. She stripped the beds. She opened every window in the house. The cold winds cut through the house furiously, and Mrs. Drimley crouched as close as she could to the measly fire in the hearth on her dirty, rugless floor. The corner of her eye betrayed a heap of haphazardly stacked knitwear, and she

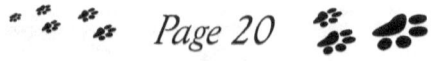

stiffly turned toward it. There, kneeling before the chair that had nearly consumed her as her father had been consumed, she sifted through the heart stitches. She could not say or think in words what the stitching had done. Mulligan knew, though.

Freshly napped, Mulligan descended from the davenport and gracefully stretched his aching back. Nonchalantly, he meandered over to shivering Mrs. Drimley.

"Why is it so cold?" Mulligan yawned.

"I'm airing the house," Mrs. Drimley absently replied. Her fingers sunk into the pile of stitching. Mr. Drimley had brought that yarn to her after a particularly good day at the fish market. Now she had a moss stitched, cream colored shawl. A purple mitten in stockinette. A navy one in seed. A geranium pink cable scarf so generously long it would still drag the floor if she wrapped it around twice. Socks in every color and pattern, but none the same. *What could I have been thinking,* she silently wondered.

"Clearly you weren't, my lady," Mulligan said, matter of factly.

Mrs. Drimley started and stared at the cat who stared regally right back at her.

"Thinking," Mulligan clarified, "You weren't thinking, and no wonder. I'm not sure it matters, though, as all these pieces will keep you warm, matching or not."

Mrs. Drimley considered, for a moment, this cat who had just read her mind. At first she felt sure she must

immediately dismiss the creature, who seemed to not know his place in nature with his talking and his knowing and his reasoning. But he was right. And he did provide the fish every day. Mrs. Drimley looked Mulligan up and down, considering how dangerous it might be to keep a mind-reading cat with a decided opinion in the house. Then she shrugged. How would she get the fish if she turned the cat away?

Mrs. Drimley took stock of her pile of warm things and began to layer them on one at a time. Substantially warmer, Mrs. Drimley rose to check her water. That day she scrubbed and swept and wiped until her house gleamed. Then, after eating her stew and washing the dishes, she bathed for the first time in months. And when she laid down that night in freshly washed bedding, in her aired-out house, smelling of the powder Mr. Drimley had bought her for their last anniversary, not a single tear dampened the pillow. Even the ache in her heart was more of a steady gale than a raging storm.

An Unfortunate Encounter with Winter

One unfortunate day in January, Mulligan went out to fetch the fish. He was gone for a very long time. Mrs. Drimley was pacing on the hearthstones when she heard the tell-tale phlunk, phlunk, phlunk that let her know he had dropped the fish at the door. She raced to let him in. The sight that met her eyes filled her with horror. There laid Mulligan with the three fish, all four creatures covered densely in flaky frost. The fish were frozen solid. Mrs. Drimley was thankful when she scooped Mulligan up and wrapped him in her shawl to find that he was not as stiff as the fish. And he was still breathing, though the breaths were slow and shallow.

Hypothermia. Frostbite. Amputation. Horrible thoughts ran through Mrs. Drimley's mind as she knelt before the hearth, laid Mulligan on the warm stones, and began to rub and stroke warmth back into his body. She chided herself for allowing him to go out on this day. They'd woken to windows and doors that had been frozen completely

over after a night of howling storms. The day was still. The sun was bright. The sky clear. In other words, it was unthinkably cold. For this far north in the depths of winter, the sun is not felt regardless of how brightly she shines. And Mulligan had gone to the freezing sea.

He did not move. Not for hours. He simply kept his breathing slow and steady. His body warmed steadily, but he did not open his eyes. Mrs. Drimley stayed by his side, completely forgetting the fish outside the door, and the dinner that would not be prepared.

When her faithful watch had drawn long into the later, darker hours of the afternoon, Mrs. Drimley's eyelids began to droop, and her head began to nod and bob before her. She still knelt on the floor, both hands lying on the cat she'd just now noticed was beautiful, and struggled to stay awake. A glisten at the corner of Mulligan's closed eye shook her to attention.

"What is it?" Mrs. Drimley started out of her fatigue.

Mulligan lay motionless.

"Are you awake?" Mrs. Drimley demanded, "For heaven's sake, put me out of my misery! Will you stay or will you die?"

Mulligan heaved a sigh, "I shall live. I fear there is a problem with my right eye, though. I still cannot feel it. I cannot bear to open it. Blindness would be unbearable. You don't know what my sight means to me!"

Mrs. Drimley quickly considered what her eyesight

meant to her, and immediately recalled the vision of her Mr. Drimley in the woods, whistling that first winter day. She immediately softened her tone.

"Now, Mulligan. Open your eyes, and we will find out together. If you are blind, I will care for you. If you are not, then life will simply go on."

Mulligan still hesitated. It's a horrible thing to be on the precipice of change. Particularly when the change seems potentially devastating. To leap and find out, or to keep the eyes shut tight? Mulligan cannot be blamed for holding his eyes shut all the tighter. But he could not stay at the hearth, motionless forever, and so, while his heart raced nearly out of his chest, he bravely, slowly opened his eyes and lifted his head for a look around.

To his left everything was as it always had been, but on his right all was a blur. And his eye ached.

"Well?" Mrs. Drimley prodded.

"I can see. But not at all clearly to my right. Something has happened," Mulligan soberly reported.

Mrs. Drimley studied the cat. "There must be something we can do. For now, just rest. Would you like to move to the cushion? You may be more comfortable there with my shawl."

Mulligan agreed. Mrs. Drimley hurried to the kitchen after taking several of the shawls from her own shoulders to tuck snugly around him, for she'd suddenly realized that her patient would be hungry and nothing was prepared

to feed him. She dug the fish out from under the fresh inches of snow that had floated in during the afternoon and wondered what to do with them. It was far too late for the stew she'd made faithfully every day, and the fish were frozen solid.

Mulligan laid on the cushion woefully. He was glad that he could see, but how horrible to have to see half the world as a blur for the rest of his life! He was not pleased, and he was enjoying wallowing in his misery.

But the racket coming from the kitchen was making it seriously difficult to be woebegone. Curiosity was getting the better of him, and that was aggravating. Could he not just have his moment of distress? A cat deserved some time to grieve his eyesight, didn't he?

Mulligan struggled to stay downtrodden. But it did not last long. He sulkily slunk off the sofa and made his way to the kitchen. The blurriness made his travel different than usual. He felt disoriented, but not lost. He stopped short in the doorway to watch Mrs. Drimley frantically scurry around waving a pan here and a vegetable there. It was dizzying to watch her. She looked out of her mind. Watching the scene half in focus and half in a hazy blur added to the confusion Mulligan was experiencing. Mrs. Drimley gave something in the pan a flourished flip and then went back to haphazardly chopping another something on a cutting board.

Mulligan took in the view and then decided it was

more polite for him to make his presence known with a tactfully executed, "Ahem."

"Oh!" Mrs. Drimley nervously tittered, "Uh, here, try this. It's a little something different."

Mrs. Drimley spooned out a bit of brothy sauce onto Mulligan's saucer. Mulligan inspected it thoroughly with his one good eye, and then turned the same eye up to Mrs. Drimley who stood expectantly over him, hands clasped together as if in prayer. Mulligan dutifully bent down and lapped a quick lap at the sauce in the saucer. Then he greedily slurped up the rest of the sauce.

A fire lit in Mrs. Drimley's eyes as she turned to spoon out some more sauce for Mulligan. This time she added some bits of fish and vegetable. And she fixed a plate for herself as well. Neither of them had tasted anything like this deliciousness. They tried to eat daintily and failed. Upon failing, they completely gave into themselves and ate with abandon. Hoggishly. They left the dishes where they lay and plopped themselves into the living room.

"How will we ever eat stew again?" Mrs. Drimley managed to say, though her thoroughly stuffed stomach protested any movement whatsoever.

Mulligan, who had barely made it back to his cushion without dragging his belly on the ground and who was now lying shamelessly on his back with all his paws sprawled wildly replied, "We couldn't ever."

The Eyepiece, the Rug, and
the Problem with the Post

But they did. Habit is mightily determined, and does not make way for newness without a fight. The way things were changing so rapidly, it's no wonder Mrs. Drimley slipped sleepily into her cooking routine nearly immediately after a brief foray into deliciousness.

Instead of spending time on creative cooking, Mrs. Drimley had scoured the house looking for Mr. Drimley's catalog. She'd had an idea about Mulligan's bad eye. It had been several weeks and still, his sight in his right eye had not improved. The pain was gone, but the blurry vision was not. Mrs. Drimley was succumbing to the reality that Mulligan would not regain his original vision, which was truly unfortunate.

If she could only find those catalogs she would be able to search for an eyepiece for her cat. Mr. Drimley had ordered eye glasses when the letters on the pages of his beloved books began to blur. He'd sent off for them at the

post office in town and then had picked them up there when he'd gone to market.

Her search became more and more frantic, and soon she'd turned the house inside out. I'm afraid that her fervor was fed by more than concern over her cat's eyesight. This whole predicament was making her think of things she'd never thought about before. Namely, about all the things she did not know. There was the problem of the post—she did not know the way there, the way to the market in town, the way to town even! Why, in all those years, did she never go to town? She'd preferred the house, but, oh, she could kick herself now for hiding away.

Mrs. Drimley began to stamp around the house. Why in the world did Mr. Drimley hide those catalogs away like this? Why hadn't he just kept them somewhere obvious? That man had never been able to keep track of anything, always wandering about, never telling her anything. She knew nothing about the management of things outside of cleaning the house and preparing food. Her anger wrestled with panic. How in the world was she going to survive without Mr. Drimley to take care of things? She'd needed no money yet, but surely she would. The need for an eyepiece for Mulligan had reminded her of this, too. And what if a window cracked, or the chimney needed clearing, or...there were too many things to consider in detail.

Mrs. Drimley stood in a total rage in front of Mr. Drimley's bureau. She hadn't gone near it yet. Standing there, her

mind raced from one thought to another. *I mustn't move his things or he'll be looking for them. That's crazy talk, Elsie, he's gone. Gone, gone. He'll never touch these things again.* Tears welled up her eyes making her vision go blurry. Her anger hadn't subsided yet, and she clung to it for dear life. *Don't leave me now, or I'll be back in that chair,* she thought. She gripped the drawer pulls that Mr. Drimley had carved into seagulls and fitted himself on the second drawer from the top. The smell overcame her first. Salty, sea air and man. That was the smell of her Mr. Drimley. Now the tears spilled over as she filled her hands with his shirts and held them to her heart. Stripes and plaids and plains, all in colors of the sea. She emptied the drawer, placing the shirts on the bed, not really knowing why. There at the bottom of the drawer, stacked tidily, was a collection of catalogs.

"Of course," Mrs. Drimley huffed. She sank onto the bed, staring blankly at the shirts.

Mulligan came slinking and stretching into the room. Clearly, he'd just finished his nap. He leapt deftly on the bed and studied the situation. Mrs. Drimley had barely lifted her head to notice him. He cleared his throat, which sounded a bit like a hiccup.

"Don't speak." Mrs. Drimley gave the order rather weakly, but there was a resoluteness that had Mulligan biting off his words and tipping his head to study her further. "Don't speak, and don't sit there philosophizing. Just be an ordinary cat for a moment."

Mulligan considered his knowledge of ordinary cats. It was not very expansive. He had vague recollections of his brother and sister kittens tumbling through straw with each other, but certainly that was not what Mrs. Drimley had in mind. He flipped through his memory to find the few memories of his exhausted mother. She groomed any kitten she could get her paws on relentlessly.

Very well, thought Mulligan rather superiorly, and then he abjectly began to lick Mrs. Drimley's nearest hand. He felt very awkward trying to behave like an ordinary cat, and it vexed him to obey her orders. Still, Mrs. Drimley seemed so agitated and something must be done.

The soft, scratchy licks had taken Mrs. Drimley by surprise. She raised her eyebrows high as she studied Mulligan dutifully behaving like a cat, yet obviously dubious about the action. The absurdity of this cat trying to be a cat unleashed a trickle of humor in the lady's belly which soon erupted in a volcano of laughter. Mrs. Drimley fell onto her bed and laughed so raucously that Mulligan was sure she'd lost her mind. First the stamping around that had woken him and now this?

Mulligan marched over to where Mrs. Drimley had sprawled herself on the bed and tried to sound stately, "Pull yourself together, Lady!"

Mrs. Drimley gave Mulligan one sharp glance that glinted around the edges with humor and sorrow, "Oh,

hush, you," she said, which made Mulligan grin from ear to ear.

Mrs. Drimley bolted suddenly up and scooped Mr. Drimley's shirts into her arms. She carried them through the hall and up the stairs into the frigid second floor. She made her way down the shadowed hall, ignoring all the closed doors, save one to her right. It creaked and hesitated to be opened after months of damp disuse. She'd oil the hinges, if she could find the oil, she thought ruefully. For now, she gave the door a hearty shove and then felt her way into the familiar room.

She found the lamp on the table where she'd left it, and lit it with the matches that were always in her apron pocket. As the light grew she took a satisfied look around the room. Dusty from disuse, as it had been downstairs, but still beautiful. The table, large and clear, save the lamp, two heavily draped floor-to-ceiling windows bookending the cushioned rocking chair.

And the large cupboard full of fabric, threads, hooks and needles of all sizes for all uses pushed squarely against the wall. Accumulated over years of holidays and birthdays and just because days. These had been her most treasured gifts from Mr. Drimley. She'd rearrange the cupboard from time to time. The newness was thrilling, and imposing. Of course, she'd used fabric and notions from time to time when she or Mr. Drimley were in need of some new thing, but as a general rule, she couldn't bear to cut into the

perfect squares of fabric unless it was absolutely necessary. She would not need to cut into her new fabric for this project, though. She dropped Mr. Drimley's shirts onto the table and picked up the one whose elbows she'd repaired numerous times. It had a stain on the lapel that had been too stubborn to be scrubbed away. He'd loved this shirt. Mrs. Drimley buried her face into that lapel for the briefest moment, and then, ripped with all her might. Once that shirt have been made into strips, she set to work on the next and the next and the next shirt until all that remained was a pile of strips of fabric and the remnants of collars, cuffs, and buttons.

This had taken a considerable amount of effort, and Mrs. Drimley was exhausted. Still, she took three of the strips and began braiding them together. She wanted to at least begin the next phase of this project before she went down to make and eat supper. With one length of braid complete, Mrs. Drimley left her project in process and wearily went down the stairs. It was when she reached the living room that she noticed the bare floor. *There,* she thought. *I'll put the rug there.*

The Thaw

Winter melted slowly that year. Spring never comes in the same way twice. This year it came in fits and starts. Spring should always be beautiful with its flowers and fresh greens, but some years it simply is not. This year it was all gusts and mud interspersed with the leftover flurries that Lord Winter would not save for next year. The sharp greens and jagged branches, with no piles of snow to soften them, assaulted the senses.

Mrs. Drimley's spirits responded accordingly. Every day she braided and sewed. Every day the rug got bigger. Every day she drew closer to the necessity of leaving the house, for she'd found the ad she'd been looking for. She'd only need to send money to an address with a letter describing her needs, and an eyepiece would be had.

Mulligan watched all this with extensive curiosity. He was in favor of the idea of an eyepiece, for his sight had not improved. It took considerable energy to be constantly judging whether the blur to his right was a shadow or a

table leg. Not to mention, the chore of catching fish was made all the more tedious by his impairment.

Alas, he was growing listless from the droning sameness of winter life. Mrs. Drimley had been awfully quiet since she'd begun the rug. He'd find her muttering sometimes, and when he inquired after her thoughts she sent him coldly away.

There were moments when Mrs. Drimley was softer. She'd offer him a pat on the head, a scratch behind the ears. It would not last long. Her eyes would grow wistful and she'd be off, back up to the cold room, braiding and sewing with a blank look in her eyes. It was like the knitting, but different. This time, Mrs. Drimley was thinking. Mulligan could almost see the gears turning in her head. He knew they weren't flowery, delightful thoughts. They were bare branch thoughts, and they were scratching at her insides. Regardless, the cold floor would have a rug. Just in time for Spring when they wouldn't really need it. Isn't that the way? Oh well, it would be there come next winter, and they would be glad to have it then.

Within her cold exterior, Mrs. Drimley's wheels most certainly were turning in agitating ways. As is the case when all sap begins to flow, there is no real evidence that it will ever be productive. Don't you think that after a whole season of lying dormant, that a tree feels uncomfortable when the warmer weather begins to stir its resources from root to branch? It must feel like waking up from a sleep

when your head or your arm was turned the wrong way. Well, Mrs. Drimley had been asleep for a long, long, long time. And as she began to awaken, she wondered if she'd ever been awake before at all. After forty-some years of being alive, this is a discomforting thought. The first sap that began to flow was icy cold, in icy veins.

There were days that Mrs. Drimley tried to forget. She tried to forget that Mr. Drimley was dead and that she'd collected the measly pile of firewood and begun to think things she'd never thought before. She wanted to wake up one day and find that nothing had changed. She thought she could gladly go on doing the same things she'd always done for the rest of her life. If things could be like before, she could be content again. She had been content in the sameness. And now, it had all been stolen away. Thoughts came unbidden, rising up from a bubbling stream somewhere deep inside. She wished she'd never thought them. She wished she still did not know the stream was there. On the days when it was quiet, she ignored it while she braided and sewed the shirts he'd never wear again, and let herself drift away to a dreamland that would never be all there was again. Carrying the firewood. Boiling the water. Stripping the beds. Airing the house.

Time for Mrs. Drimley was running out. Her hiding-out days were nearly over. She was going to have to decide how she would go to town; with despair in her heart or determination? This is not an easy choice, my friends.

Certainly You Could Do It

"I've fixed a basket for you, Mulligan."

Mulligan tiptoed nonchalantly to the basket. His sensitivity had been pricked raw by the sharp coldness that had reigned over his interactions with Mrs. Drimley for the past several weeks. Naturally, he was suspicious about this sudden wave of sweetness. He suspected ulterior motives.

He suspected right.

In the basket was a whole fish, a new, miniature cushion which had clearly been hastily sewn, and a bowl of the fresh spring berries Mulligan had been enjoying immensely, in a very un-catlike way and were soon to go out of season.

Mulligan looked from the basket to Mrs. Drimley with a cool countenance, "How and to where am I to carry this? Am I getting the boot?"

"Heavens, no!" Mrs. Drimley said with forced excitement and a nervous titter, "I just thought you'd love to go into town and order that new eyepiece yourself. Of course

you couldn't go without a dinner, and the cushion is there in case you need a nap on the way home."

Mulligan blinked blankly at Mrs. Drimley. "And I am to carry the basket? How?"

"We'll tie it to your back. That's what Mr. Drimley always did."

"My good lady," Mulligan cleared his throat and approached the topic carefully, "I am not Mr. Drimley. And I cannot go into town."

"Why not? You'll have fun! You've moped around here for weeks."

"*I've* moped?" Mulligan took a steadying breath. "Mrs. Drimley. Just what, exactly, do you think they'd do with a talking cat in town? It's ludicrous to think I could go there, let alone carry this basket." Mulligan huffed.

"I'll give you two fish."

"I'll catch my own fish if I'm hungry."

Mrs. Drimley stamped her foot.

"Certainly you could do it if you wanted to," Mrs. Drimley pouted, "and you would if you loved me."

Mulligan sat firmly on his haunches. "Now you're just getting desperate. Go or don't go to town. I never asked for an eyepiece; that was your idea," though he winced a bit inside at the thought of not having one. "I won't be manipulated."

Mrs. Drimley dropped to the ground feeling defeated, and sheepish. It's a sorry thing to realize you've tried to manipulate your cat.

"Maybe there is a way to avoid town. We made it through the first fall and winter, certainly we could find a way."

Mulligan thought disparagingly about the pantry which was growing barer every day.

Mrs. Drimley seemed to read his thoughts. Her shoulders sagged considerably, and she sat looking so defeated that Mulligan took pity on her.

"My dear Mrs. Drimley, there will only ever be one first time. And it will have to be done. Better just get on with it. You won't get a better day." Mulligan nudged her with his nose. "Come, let's exchange this fish for a nice hunk of yesterday's loaf. You'll be off and back again before you know it. Then you can tell me all about your adventure when you get home."

Mulligan continued to talk as he nudged Mrs. Drimley along as she went through the motions of packing the basket in the same manner she used to pack it for Mr. Drimley. She strapped the basket onto her back, making sure that the eyepiece advertisement was tucked well into the basket. Soon, she found she had been nudged right to the edge of the cliff next to the flagpole Mr. Drimley had driven into the ground years ago. Mrs. Drimley had not thought to take down the flag as Mr. Drimley had diligently done every year before. Now she saw that it was a tattered remnant of what it had been, and the bright sea greens had faded dreadfully from the winter winds.

Mrs. Drimley never ventured farther than the path that

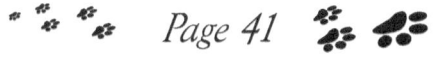

looped around the front of the house facing the sea. That is how she found herself, at the middle of her life, after living nearly twenty eight years by the sea, seeing its shore for the first time in her life.

"Now, be careful as you go," Mulligan intoned, "though if I can do it, surely you can. And when you come back, look for the flag. It will guide you home."

Mrs. Drimley looked skeptically at the jagged rocks along the cliff wall as she considered her apparel. The long skirt was going to be a problem. She quickly gathered it up in knots here and there to free her feet for movement.

"Do or die," was all she said before she set herself into motion.

Determination

Now, this was the first moment that determination won in Mrs. Drimley's heart, and something always happens when you let determination defeat despair. The unfortunate truth, though, is that determination must defeat despair over and over and over. It is not a one time sort of battle.

Mrs. Drimley found this out the second she was clinging to the side of the cliff. Her determination fell straight down to the crashing waves below. She glanced quickly down to where she saw a boat, still mercifully tied. Then she turned her terrified eyes to Mulligan who eyed her steadily. Mrs. Drimley drew a fresh bucket of determination up from her guts and began to carefully lower herself down the cliff. Once she was moving, she realized that the going was made fairly easy by the well-defined platforms in the rocks.

She had a moment of dizziness when she glanced up. Mulligan's head now looked like a button high up on the

cliff. She started to shriek out an order for him not to fall down, for heaven's sake, when she realized that he'd been up and down the cliff daily for months and months. With a shrug of her shoulders to redistribute the weight in the basket, Mrs. Drimley continued down the cliff.

She glanced around once she'd reached the thick blanket of stones that covered the shore. Because it made moving easier, she left her skirts tied the way they were and made her way along to the wide post to which the boat was tied. She watched the energetic waves, aghast, and looked at the upside-down boat, which looked more like a rickety mess than a sea faring vessel. She inspected it closely, not knowing really what she was looking for other than holes. When she was satisfied, she heaved the whole contraption over and drug it down to the water. After that struggle, she was pleased that the boat was small enough to be handled by one person. She eyed it suspiciously as it rode the waves.

She pushed it out further, and effectively soaked her skirts. She did not know whether she was surprised or not that the boat continued to float. It was much harder to maneuver now that her clothing had become weighted with water, but she trudged up to shore and gathered her basket, which she'd secured to the docking pole. She picked up the worn oars that had been safely tucked under tarp and boat, and made her way back out to the boat.

Though she made noteworthy attempts, it was im-possible

to gracefully climb into the bobbing boat. She gathered her skirts this way and that; tried lifting her leg just so, and then finally succumbed to rolling her way into the boat.

Mrs. Drimley was sprawled face down with her middle folding over the rowing bench. Her head pounding as the blood rushed in. She forced her eyes open so she could get her bearings and set herself upright without capsizing the dory. As she firmly planted her hands and began to waggle toward kneeling, she glanced up and saw an old, green bottle with a wide base and a long skinny neck. It was cloudy, no doubt from the salty sea. As the boat tipped with her movement, the bottle rolled right down to her hand.

She grasped it and gingerly sat herself aright. Upon a closer look at the bottle, Mrs. Drimley saw it was the container for a rolled up note. Mrs. Drimley shook the bottle to retrieve the paper. Her hands shook. The wind was fierce, and it was so much colder by the water than she had expected. It did not help that she was soaking wet. When the tip of the paper was close enough to catch on the end of her finger, Mrs. Drimley gingerly slid it out of the bottle. It was almost crisp from the moist, salty air, and she took great care as she unrolled it.

She recognized the writing immediately as Mr. Drimley's.

My Dear Elsa Dora,

If you're reading this, it most likely means I am gone or too ill

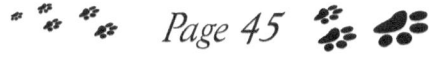

to speak. This is a "just in case" letter, and I do hope you'll never be in need of it. But if you're here it most likely means you need to get to town without me, and I'll have to warn you. The sea way is treacherous, and you must be careful. Set the boat straight out to sea and row past the waves. You'll have to row mightily. Then you'll need to go west about five miles. You'll see the bay. Make toward the landing there. That's where all the folks are. You can't miss it. Always keep the shoreline in easy sight. Don't venture out too far. Of course, you could go by foot. It'll take you a good long time, the shore way, though. Anyways, I'm not here to stop you or help you or send you any other way, so that's the way by the sea if you're determined to take it.

Mist gathered in Mrs. Drimley's eyes and she dabbed it away. Fat lot of good this would do her, she thought, though her heart was echoing sadness on top of the fear she was already swallowed up in. She eyed the ramshackle boat, and she eyed the shore and wondered what had possessed Mr. Drimley to plant roots in such a place and why in the world she'd not thought twice about following him here. She gave herself some lenience, knowing that they'd come through the woods, which she understood.

Her eyes stretched out to the horizon as she gripped the oars with all her might. She was just going to have to learn to understand the sea.

Mulligan, On His Own

Mulligan watched Mrs. Drimley fumble with the boat and the oars. She was not the most graceful boatswoman he could imagine, but she did manage. There were several false starts before Mrs. Drimley was able to climb aboard with her wet skirts, ridiculous things, and then successfully row over the incoming waves. Mulligan watched Mrs. Drimley's attempts with interest. First naïve, then irritated, then despondent, then determined. The waves and the boats did not defeat Mrs. Drimley, but Mulligan could not help being anxious for her return home. She'd make it, he had no doubt, but what scrapes might she get in? He'd have to put it out of his mind and go on faith for the day. His worries weren't going to help one little bit.

Once she was well on her way, Mulligan resolutely turned back toward the house. The spring air was invigorating. It reminded him that he was a young thing. His fur blew wildly and he twisted and turned into the wind so that every inch of his skin could catch a fresh breath.

Then he made his way down the path, first with great poise, but the spring beauty got the best of him and sent him frolicking down the path so lightly that he nearly forgot who he was: an odd, speaking cat, in the charge of—or in charge of, he couldn't quite figure out which—one grieving widow with only the most rudimentary life skills.

Never mind that for the day. Mulligan threw himself down on the ground and laid looking up at the sky. The clouds flew by with the breeze, a large fluffy ball here and there, but mostly wisps and swirls. Mulligan rolled in the dusty path, snuck through the new, delicate grass, pounced at ants, and batted at a swarm of gnats. As the sun rose toward late morning, he found a sunny spot to dream in. His mind was on the eyepiece. How much more lovely would this spring day be if half of it were not a blur! And he was not ashamed to say that he was looking forward to being so distinguished looking. Imagine. A cat with an eyepiece! Oh yes, he was going to be grand.

Though, just an eyepiece might look a bit bare, he began to think. A dapper wardrobe. A selection of scarves. A hat, just so. Just what a cat with an eyepiece needed. Plans to laze and dream in the sun all day were completely forgotten. Mulligan sat himself upright and made steady work of putting his fur to rights, which was unkempt and full of dust after his morning of frivolity. Bathing was not the most pleasant task for a cat, but Mulligan was dutiful about it. There was no sense in having Mrs. Drimley all in

an uproar as soon as she got home over dusty paw prints all over her kitchen floor.

Once Mulligan was presentable again, he took himself inside and headed straight up the stairs to the second floor. He nudged open the door to Mrs. Drimley's work room and saw that the rug had grown large while the pile of shirt strips was now very small. *Good,* thought Mulligan, a project nearly finished. He marched over the rug towards the cupboard full of fabrics and all manners of tools to make soft things. The cupboard towered over him. He had a moment of disorientation when he looked up at the intricately carved patterns of vines and leaves and flowers on the door. He wondered if Mr. Drimley had made the cupboard; that was most likely. It glistened, in the one stream of sunlight sneaking through a crack in the heavy curtains. *How did she work in this dark room?* Mulligan wondered.

He huffed in the direction of the curtains. He'd take care of them in just a minute. First, he used his nose to coax a crack of an opening out of the cupboard door. Then he swung the door wide with his paw and walked it around until it clattered against the wall. He quickly performed the same tricks to open the matching door on the right, which was a bit trickier, given the challenge of working around his blurry vision. Now, wide open, Mulligan inspected the contents of the cupboard. It was a magical wonderland of possibilities, he thought. It was hard to see, though, on account of the darkness and his eye.

Gripping the corner of the drapes in his teeth, he pulled mightily to let the sun into the room. It took a bit of thinking and doing to find a way to keep the curtains away from the windows since the curtain hooks on the wall were puny and made for ribbon tie backs, rather than to catch the drapes wholly. One set of curtains, he tucked behind the opened cupboard door. This required much maneuvering, and no small amount of good timing, but he eventually managed. The other set of curtains, he dragged widely around the rocking chair. It wasn't as bright as he'd prefer, but it was better than before. Less tidy, but Mulligan needed to see, and he couldn't very well light the lantern with no thumbs, now, could he?

Mulligan's attention turned back to the cupboard now that he could see it a little better. A gleam came into his eye, and then he dived in.

The First Trip

Mrs. Drimley was certain she'd never been more terrified in her entire life. What was she doing out here, riding the swells in complete and utter agony? The moment she'd made it out past the waves she'd had another moment of panic. She thought of turning back, but she was still surging with the determination she'd used to fuel her arms with rowing power. She followed Mr. Drimley's directions. She headed south. She stayed within safe eyeshot of the shore. Then she saw it, along the shoreline, a cluster that simply looked different. The shoreline changed from cliffs to more level ground as she rowed.

Mrs. Drimley rowed steadily toward the cluster which gradually began to take shape. It was a dock and many boats were tied to it. Some had sails, but most were like hers. Mrs. Drimley began to wonder how many people she'd be interacting with. It had been years since she'd seen anyone besides Mr. Drimley. Her experience with people was limited to her cruel siblings, her father, and Mr. Drimley.

She braced herself to receive orders, for this could be a town full of people like her family. To her, Mr. Drimley, with his mild manners, had been a rarity. Her heart thudded in her chest until she thought it was sure to thump right out, but still she rowed. She drew from her well of determination over and over again. It was all she could do. It was what she must do. Mr. Drimley was gone and supplies would have to be gotten. Plus, she had promised Mulligan an eyepiece. It was the least she could do.

Rowing to the dock took much less time than Mrs. Drimley would have liked, though she did appreciate the rest that came from rowing with the waves instead of against them. She was so busy struggling to gently glide the little boat next to the dock rather than crash into it that she didn't notice the crowd of men watching at the head of the dock.

She'd nearly succeeded in her task when a particularly forceful wind came along and heaved her boat aggressively under the dock. Mrs. Drimley dropped the oars and grasped the landing of the dock with her elbows while her legs gripped the seat of the boat. Though she grunted and pulled with all her might she could not pull the boat even partially out from under the dock. She hung on tight and thought about her next move.

As she weighed her options, she heard heavy footsteps falling steadily toward her. She glanced up out of the corner of her eyes. Towering over her was a grey-bearded,

weather-worn man covered shoulder to ankle in ragged clothes made of rough cloth—all in shades of white, tan, and grey. His heavy boots had been recently oiled and they smelled so terrible that Mrs. Drimley now had to add cautious breathing to her current predicament.

"Ye've got yerself in a muddle, there ma'am," said the stranger.

"Well, yes," Mrs. Drimley replied flatly.

"I'd say yer best bet is to let go and toss me your rope as you come t'other side," he advised in a slow, methodical drone.

"Yes, I think that will do," Mrs. Drimley agreed. She loosed the grip of her elbows first and dropped as fast as she could straight down into the boat to avoid a collision between her head and the dock. She simply laid in the boat as it coasted below the dock. The way the sun shone through the slats soothed her aching mind and muscles. Once her feet felt the full sun upon coming out the other side of the dock, Mrs. Drimley scrambled to grab hold of the rope. She sat up and tossed the thick, shaggy rope toward the thick, shabby man who was waiting for her. He heaved the boat and tied it to the dock, then waited as Mrs. Drimley hoisted herself and her basket out of the boat.

To Market

The relief of having made it safely to town only lasted for a moment. Mrs. Drimley was satisfied with herself as she stepped off of the dock. Overly satisfied, even. Yet, each step she took along the path that would soon bend toward the main market street, as the dock keeper had described, seemed to deflate the air in Mrs. Drimley's shoulders. She did not notice the birdsong or the light flitting through the tree leaves. She did not even notice that she was in a woods. She was only aware of her own body, bent small, eyes wary.

How many years had it been since she'd been among people other than Mr. Drimley? She could hardly think, let alone remember such a detail with her mind gone numb with panic. Her steps became infinitesimal, so grand was her dread of the people who would surely overwhelm her the moment she stepped off of the short, wooded walk.

In spite of her tortoise pace, she found herself at the edge of the wood much sooner than she wished to. As her

eyes adjusted to the full sun, she glanced around in shock. This was not the bustling marketplace Mr. Drimley had described all those years by the fire. This was a few falling-down stands with drably dressed people standing behind a measly array of offers. The market seemed to be colorless. Not a square of bright cloth or yarn, only rough looking wool that had seen no dye and had been uncreatively woven. Pitiful produce dotted one stall. A butcher hacked away at a carcass unceremoniously. It was all ghastly. Is this where Mr. Drimley had come all these years?

It wasn't until Mrs. Drimley drew her eyes up from the ramshackle market stands that she noticed the peering eyes that fixed on her. In the eyes of the women, she saw fear. In the eyes of the men, she saw disdain. Mrs. Drimley glanced down at her colorful wardrobe and her hitched up skirt, then compared them to the mud and slate hues that the other women in the market wore. Where in the world had Mr. Drimley found the goods that filled her cupboard of treasures?

Mrs. Drimley was approaching a tiny congregation of women near the produce stand to ask for directions to the post office when a line of individuals paraded into the market street. They were aligned like a row of ducks with the father at the head of the line, the mother behind him with a small child in her arms, and a row of children in descending height following behind her.

Mrs. Drimley had never wished for children of her own.

Her own dismal childhood had left her with no desire to recreate the experience, and looking at these children, Mrs. Drimley was pleased with her decision. They were the dullest and drabbest children you can imagine. Not a smile to be seen on any of the seven faces. Even the baby in the mother's arms stared blankly at Mrs. Drimley. Only the father had any expression on his face. The demanding smugness that radiated from his stare was not pleasant at all. Mrs. Drimley immediately set herself against him. He appeared to find no pleasure in her presence either.

The family's arrival had left the already muffled noise of the market nearly silent. Though their presence could not stop the birds from singing, not a word was spoken and all human eyes fixed themselves to the ground. All except Mrs. Drimley's.

It had taken her years after meeting Mr. Drimley for the first time in the woods around her childhood home to look him in the eye. Once she began to meet his eyes, she saw that she mattered, too. Gradually, she had forgotten the years of never looking up at anyone or anything. She could not go back to looking down now.

The father marched directly toward her until they stood face to face. His eyes were demanding, but Mrs. Drimley had no idea what of. She'd been struck dumb and found herself frozen. Still, she did not waver.

Reader, there is something you should know. Sometimes, what we don't know makes us stronger. Sometimes,

all of our experiences bubble up into one perfect moment that allows us to be brave. This was Mrs. Drimley's moment.

The Unexpected

"What brings you to my marketplace?" the man asked briskly.

His marketplace? Mrs. Drimley wondered. He was smiling, but his smile felt like ice. Mr. Drimley's smile had felt like wool, warm and scratchy. Mrs. Drimley did not trust this man.

"I've come to send for goods from the post office."

"What could you need that you cannot find here in this fine marketplace?" The man gestured broadly around as though he was surrounded by an array of desirable goods. Not that you couldn't get by on the goods in the marketplace. You certainly could. It appeared that all the people, besides Mrs. Drimley, who were standing in the market at that very moment did survive on those meager offerings. Mrs. Drimley, however, had been living on more, and so she saw the market for what it was.

"My needs are not your concern. Where will I find the post office, sir?"

The man balked, and the people squirmed in their places.

After a moment of frigid silence, the man replied, "You will find it a quarter of a mile from here if you follow this road."

He swallowed hard and worked his hands into fists. When he turned and took broad, heavy strides toward the market vendors, the line of his family followed. Mrs. Drimley's eyes caught the eyes of this man's wife only for a second, and she nearly gasped. The slightest twist of the head and the threat in her eyes kept Mrs. Drimley from making a sound. The hollowness in her sister's cheeks, and the faint hint of a healing bruise had quickened Mrs. Drimley's heart. As she watched the line of dismal children parade before her, she turned back toward their father.

"I didn't get your name, sir," she said with force she'd never used before.

"It's Appleton. Henry Appleton. Welcome to the harbor." But Mrs. Drimley did not feel welcome, not welcome at all.

The market sellers coughed up their money readily as Mr. Appleton made his rounds. They put goods in Mrs. Appleton's basket and looked sympathetically at the children who could do no more than stare into thin air.

Mrs. Drimley hurried away from her sister, nieces, and nephews as quickly as she possibly could. She ducked off of the path and into the woods to catch her breath. Tears stung at the corners of her eyes. For the first time

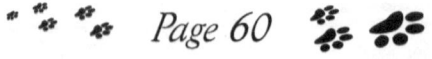

in more than two decades, her heart was back in her family's cabin—everyone screeching at her to do this and to do that, her father glued to his chair, the inescapable heaviness that suffocated her mind fell down around her. Though she was surrounded by nothing but the open air of the wilderness, she struggled to catch her breath.

The mind is a funny thing. It can make us believe we are free when we are trapped. And it can make us believe we are trapped when we are free. Right now, Mrs. Drimley's mind was performing circus acts, leaping between the past and present with such tenacity that Mrs. Drimley found herself dizzy.

It wasn't until this very moment that Mrs. Drimley felt fully what her life could have been, what Mr. Drimley had done when he'd led her to the woods and into life by the sea, and what she'd done when she'd been brave enough to follow him. She'd learned to write and read. He'd brought her books and beauty. And she had been content enough with that measure of freedom. Now, though...

Looking into the face of a woman she would not have recognized if not for the family eyes, Mrs. Drimley was shaken a little more awake. It was dreadful, but she could not unsee what she had seen. Nor could she shake the questions that were ringing through her mind.

Mrs. Drimley pulled herself together and resolutely made her way to the post office.

The Post Office

Have you ever put armor on your heart? When you've seen something or learned something that makes you want to right a wrong, a wrong that someone else is responsible for, your heart goes soft in its compassion for this wronged thing or person or animal, and then a hard armor of anger and justice forms around it so you have the guts to do what it takes to right the wrong. Well, Mrs. Drimley put armor on her heart that day in the market. The wrong thing was the way her sister and the Appleton children stared blankly out of bruised and dirty eyes. The person responsible, Mrs. Drimley was absolutely sure, was Mr. Appleton. By the time Mrs. Drimley warily climbed the rotting steps that led to the post office door, all that could be seen of her was armor on her heart. Sometimes, seeing injustice makes you strong.

The post office was not at all what Mrs. Drimley had imagined it would be. She'd imagined a sturdy building, whitewashed, with flowers growing in baskets at the

door. In fact, she nearly mistook the office for a shack, so weatherworn and poorly assembled were its planks. If not for the small placard in the window that read Postal Office she would have kept walking.

Though she was worried that the door would fall right off its hinges, she pushed it open and stepped into shimmery dust-filled air. Mrs. Drimley was not only blinded by the glittery light swathing in through the filthy windows, she was also choked by the sheer mass of dust in the air. Shameful, she thought, conveniently forgetting the months that went by with her home unattended.

It took her a moment to learn the art of breathing without coughing, about as long as it took for her eyes to adjust to the strange contrast between the golden glitter of dust in sunlight and the deadened grayness of the dusty realm outside of the sunstream.

"May I help you," croaked an ancient voice, causing Mrs. Drimley to nearly jump out of her skin.

"Eh," Mrs. Drimley cleared her throat, attempting to regain her composure. "Eh, yes. I'd like to send this in the mail. It's already addressed, but I'll need to pay for postage."

"Mmmm..." the lady muttered as she weighed the letter on a rusty scale. She shuffled around in ratty slippers and socks that sagged to show legs that looked like they should belong to a bear they were so full of thick hair. Mrs. Drimley forced her eyes upward only to see sticks and twigs in hair

that hadn't seen a comb in a century. The teeth were bad, and the face was haggard, but when she turned her eyes toward Mrs. Drimley, they were fierce and clear.

"What is it you send for?" asked the post matron.

"Oh, an eyepiece," Mrs. Drimley answered nervously.

"Eyesight bad, is it?" the lady said with a crooked smile that showed rotting teeth.

"Oh, my eyesight is fine," Mrs. Drimley responded. Why was she so nervous? She was sweating.

"Got a man to buy an eyepiece for, eh?" she said with a crude chuckle.

"No, my husband is dead. It's for my ca...ca...ca... taracts. My cataracts." Mrs. Drimley could not believe herself. *What had possessed her to nearly tell her secret?*

"Cataracts, mmm. An eyepiece for cataracts. Well I'll like seeing that when it comes in. Sent off a couple of years ago, a friend did, for an eyepiece. His time on the sea, he said, had blown his sight out to the deep," she said with a chuckle.

Mrs. Drimley's stomach twisted in a knot. "Mr. Drimley."

"Aye, yes."

"My husband."

"Hmph," she said ferociously. "I knew he was dead. Others thought maybe he'd finally stocked up enough goods to last him. But I knew he was gone. Shame. He was a good customer. Ordered things all the time." The lady was eyeing her sharply now. Sizing her up.

"Yes, last fall. It was a horrible cough that wouldn't be treated."

"Mmm."

Suddenly the shutters slapped closed, and the door slammed and locked.

"Lunchtime," was all the lady said. Then she turned and slid open a door in the floor.

A tremor ran all the way through to Mrs. Drimley's bones. For one moment she thought she'd lost it; that Mulligan and this town, her sister, and this lady were all a bad dream. Then the post matron hopped right into the hole in the floor and disappeared from sight.

Appearances are More Than What They're Made Of

Mrs. Drimley had a choice now. She could go straight home and explain to Mulligan that an eyepiece was out of the question, and that they'd have to learn to live off the land. Or, she could follow the post matron into that hole and find out what in the world was going on.

Mrs. Drimley only had a moment to make a choice, and the choice that made the most sense in that tiny fissure of time was to follow, of course. There was no graceful way to get into the hole and no telling what would happen once she was in. *Still,* she thought, *if that old lady can do it, so can I.* Mrs. Drimley scrambled down and found herself in utter darkness. She had to hunch her body over and take clomping steps forward. With her arms outstretched, she shied away from tree roots. She hoped with all her might that the scurrying pitter-pat noise she heard were not critters in this dugout cave. It had been dug, this much was clear, and it kept getting smaller and smaller. It felt

like she was in the cave for hours on end, until at last she saw a light.

When she stepped out of the tunnel, filthy from head to toe, it was into an immaculate dining room full of beauty. Mrs. Drimley had never seen such a place. There was banging in the next door room, and Mrs. Drimley hesitantly followed the noise.

She pressed the cream-colored swinging door slightly and peeked through the crack in the doorway. It was a kitchen, and there was the Postal Matron in her haggard outfit, which now looked entirely out of place in the pristine and well stocked kitchen. Shiny pots hung on yellow rose-papered walls. Dishes were stacked tidily on creamy shelves. On the stove a pot steamed, into which the post matron dipped a long-handled spoon. She slurped the contents from the spoon and gave a delighted giggle. She even did a little hop.

She's awfully spry for an old lady, Mrs. Drimley thought.

"Grab a bowl, dear, and we'll set down for a bite," The post matron said as though Mrs. Drimley had been expected, even formally invited to dinner.

"How did you know I was here?" Mrs. Drimley said, aghast.

"How does anyone know anything?" the post matron sauced, then spun around and met Mrs. Drimley's eyes full on.

Here in the full light, the matron's wrinkles showed

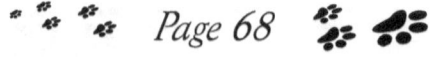

themselves to be more deeply etched than they had appeared in the dark post office. But here, the wrinkles looked stately and added to the lady's beauty, instead of making her appear frail and disgusting. Her hair was still a mess, and her outfit was in tired condition, but Mrs. Drimley felt for certain she had been duped. This was no haggard woman.

Practical lady that she was, Mrs. Drimley felt as at home as could be in this kitchen. She made her way over to the shelf with bowls and took two down. Then she plucked two spoons from the plaster chicken on the counter that had flatware instead of feathers. The postal matron had two cloth napkins and a tureen of soup at the table when Mrs. Drimley went back into the dining room.

The two ladies sat down and the postal matron filled their bowls with soup.

"Who in the world are you and where in the world are we?" Mrs. Drimley demanded.

"Rude, aren't you?" Florie replied with a cackle.

Mrs. Drimley stammered, "Well, I don't mean to be rude, but I've met my limit for oddness and I'm not sure I can accept anything at face value just now. If questions are rude, I'm afraid it's just going to have to be that way."

The postal matron let a big belly laugh bubble up from stomach. "I like you, Mrs. Drimley. What's your first name again?"

"It's Elsa."

"Well, Elsa," the postal matron sat down her spoon resolutely and did a quick internal assessment, "my name is Foralie Windshaven. You may call me Florie."

"Florie," Mrs. Drimley repeated dryly.

"Florie, yes," Foralie Windshaven replied. "The townsfolk call me Mrs. Windshaven, though I've never married. Just makes things more simple if they think I'm a widow is all."

Mrs. Drimley, being an true widow, bristled at this a bit. "That does not seem fair to actual widows, Florie," she replied.

"Oh, now. Don't fuss over it. You'd understand if you knew my whole story. The soup is getting cold, so eat up."

Mrs. Drimley followed orders. The soup was deliciously creamy. She stopped just short of licking the bowl clean.

"What delicious soup."

"Oh yes, it was delicious," said Florie, who had eaten three bowls full in the time it took Mrs. Drimley to finish one and who now had her feet propped up on the chair next to her and her head resting on the back of her chair. *Talk about rude*, Mrs. Drimley thought to herself.

"Pardon me if I treat you like a fast friend, Elsa. It's just, I feel at home with you. I know you can't be like the rest of them. Surely you have some beauty in your life, and surely you haven't had it beat out of you like those other grey folks." Florie tsk-tsked into her tea.

"By all appearances, you're one of them," Mrs. Drimley

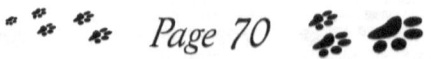

said, knowing that she'd been deceived by this "fast friend."

"Now don't get your knickers in a knot. It's pretend you have to do to survive around here. You don't want to draw attention to yourself here, Elsa, or there will be trouble. It's look down and mind your own business, that's what you'll have to do. He probably had forgotten all about you until now, I suppose."

"Who?" Mrs. Drimley demanded.

"Mr. Appleton," Florie spat out. "That horrible man. He has everyone under his thumb, that one does. Well, not me. He knows nothing of me or my real home. And because of all this," Florie held up the rags of her skirt, "and all this," then she got up and hobbled as she did in the post office, "he's never suspected a thing. I'll tell you one thing. He's not likely to come looking for you, because he's scared of the woods. That's why the tunnel is so long. Dug it straight under the woods, I did. Your Mr. Drimley was a smart one, too, he was."

"Yes," Mrs. Drimley said. There was silence while the ladies sipped their tea. Just now Mrs. Drimley was angry at her smart husband. There was so much he'd never told her, but then again, had she wanted to know? Certainly not. Mrs. Drimley sighed loudly.

"So about that eyepiece," Florie pried, "who is it for?"

"I assume there is no rule that says I must tell you about every inquiry I make by mail."

Florie chuckled.

"What I mean to say is, that's none of your business."

"Fair enough," Florie replied.

"How long will it take?"

"Several weeks, perhaps."

"Alright then. Thank you for dinner. I'll be going back now." Mrs. Drimley rose abruptly and opened the door to the tunnel which looked like a portrait instead of a door when it was closed.

However did all of this come to be? Mrs. Drimley wondered as she made her way through the tunnel. She could hear Florie puffing behind her. When she rose from the hole in the floor, she was doubly filthy as well as exhausted. *How would she ever made it back home, over the sea and up the cliff?*

By the time Mrs. Drimley had positioned herself at the post office desk, Florie was standing behind it, floor door covered without a hint or even a crack in the floorboards. She looked entirely composed, as though nothing unusual had happened at all.

"Florie."

Florie coughed. "It's Mrs. Windshaven here."

"Mrs. Windshaven," Mrs. Drimley said, annoyed. "Why go to all this effort of illusion? Why all these false appearances?"

Florie dropped her voice until it was barely audible, but the fierceness was undeniable. "Appearances are more than what they're made of. Appearances are everything in places like Appleton. These appearances give me free-

dom. Anything is worth bearing for that. Now, a gift of appearances for you," she said. She looked almost apologetically at Mrs. Drimley, then reached into her dress toward her armpit and pulled out a long stick. She flicked it directly toward Mrs. Drimley who felt nothing but a warm breeze. When she looked down, however, she saw that her appearance had been returned to the state it had been in when she'd entered the post office. Her eyes grew wide, and wider still when the shutters flew open and the door unlocked on its own.

Mrs. Drimley flew from the post office, stopping for nothing and to look at no one on her way back to her boat. She did not wait for help from the dock master. She landed directly on the rowing bench and rowed with all her might. Home. She needed to be home.

Disasterly

Well, you might as well know what Mulligan had been up to all this time, though I'm nearly ashamed to tell you. I will simply say that the entire first and second floors of the house were in disarray. Mulligan could not have cared any less about this, though. Mulligan was on cloud nine. In fact, he felt as though he was floating. You see, Mulligan had been creating all day. I can't really explain how, other than to say that a talking, thinking cat such as Mulligan is smart enough to figure out how to work scissors—even if in a rather clumsy way.

The sewing machine had been much simpler to figure out. Mulligan sat on the stool and used Mr. Drimley's old cane, gribbed between his back paws, to reach the pedal. Using his paws to guide the fabric filled Mulligan with glee. It's unexplainable. Sometimes, things that shouldn't make you deliriously happy do make you deliriously happy.

On account of the clumsy work with the scissors, I'm

sorry to say that everything Mulligan made that day was just awful. The pieces didn't align at all. Mulligan clearly did not notice this, for he'd made dozens of vests and a myriad of scarves that might have been fashionable if a cat had not cut them out.

Worst of all, he'd wasted reams of fabric trying to design a top hat that he just couldn't get right. It was this he was working at when he heard the dragging of Mrs. Drimley's feet headed in the direction of the door. *Hmph. Just when he was getting into a good rhythm,* Mulligan grumbled to himself.

He cautiously glanced around, worrying for the slightest second. Then he caught a glimpse of himself and smiled smugly. Oh, yes, he was looking good.

Mulligan pranced down the stairs, then strutted toward the kitchen. His dramatic entrance did not have the effect he was hoping for. Mrs. Drimley shoulders stayed slumped and she managed only to drop her jaw and raise a pair of tired eyebrows when she saw Mulligan.

Not to be discouraged, Mulligan stood on his hind legs and leaned on the wooden step stool in a pose he thought fashionable then asked, "So, how did it go?"

"What has happened to the place, Mulligan? Where have all these scraps come from? What is this, and how did it get here?" Mrs. Drimley said, sounding both tired and exasperated as she held up one of Mulligan's makeshift vests. "And what in the world are you wearing?"

"Isn't this green divine against my grey? I really think this color makes my eyes pop."

"MULLIGAN!" Mrs. Drimley shrieked.

"Now, there's no need to screech, woman," Mulligan replied surly.

"Mulligan," Mrs. Drimley replied taking a measuring breath. "What have you done to my supplies?" Then she was off with a panicked gasp, up the stairs, down the hall, and into her beloved room, which now held the bulk of the contents that she'd so lovingly arranged and rearranged over the past decades, all snipped to pieces. She couldn't speak. She couldn't even squeeze out the scream that wanted to come peeling from her throat. It burned, but it was stuck tight. Mulligan was dancing around the room singing the praises of the work he'd done that day, completely unaware of Mrs. Drimley's distress.

She gasped as she took in the entire scene. When her eyes landed on the empty cupboard shelves, she felt herself, for the second time that day, back in her childhood home. The owner of nothing precious, no secret treasure, nothing to admire.

Mrs. Drimley clutched the still prancing Mulligan around the belly, and plopped him into the hall. She shut the door on his confused face. Ignoring Mulligan's cries and pawing at the door, Mrs. Drimley crawled around the floor, gathering the bits and scraps, scraping them into a pile. Then she nestled, curled up a in a ball, right in the

middle of what was left of her treasure trove and slept until she could sleep no more.

Temporary Life Paralysis

Change is hard for some people. There is no doubt about this. Even little changes are hard. Big changes are another thing entirely. And when the big changes come back to back to back, it can be nearly impossible to survive. If you've never experienced many big changes right in a row with barely a chance to breathe between, let me tell you, it's just awful. You don't get to stay the same.

When Mrs. Drimley awoke the next morning in her bed of scraps, it was with a weary mind. Her body did not want to move. She tried to move. When she grew alarmed that her arms and legs would not do what she intended, she thought very deliberately, *I am going to move my fingers now,* and even that didn't work. Has this ever happened to you? It's happened to me, reader. It's called being paralyzed by life. And remember this if it ever does happen to you: it's only temporary.

There are moments in life when, in order to live with yourself, you must act. Even if you don't really know what

you are doing. Mrs. Drimley, lying on the floor, thought only of her sister, and the row of children. She had not thought of them—any of them, her siblings, her father— for a long time. She had ceased to care. It never occurred to her that they may be suffering somewhere. Surely, they, who were far more powerful than her, would be better off than she'd become. Yesterday, she'd seen proof that this was not true. Not true at all.

Mrs. Drimley tried her fingers again. She felt the slightest movement in her first finger on her right hand. Mrs. Drimley stared up at the ceiling. Had she ever really looked at this ceiling before? She imagined the room as she had seen it the night before. She thought of the bare cupboard.

Mrs. Drimley thought about crying. It seemed, though, that her tears had dried up. Her sadness was a desert now. Hot. Dry. Heavy. And hopeless. The kind of sadness that makes you shrug your shoulders and say, oh well. The kind of sadness that makes you give up on something.

I cannot be sure, but I think the thing that Mrs. Drimley gave up on that day was the hope of ever crawling back into her cocoon. The cocoon was her life with Mr. Drimley. The life in which she never had to leave her house. The life in which she knew nothing of town and all its grayness, her sister with her dirty bunch of children, or of Florie. The life in which she'd believed everything Mr. Drimley had told her and had never questioned what

he was not saying. That was Mrs. Drimley's cocoon. And it was leaving her.

What I can be sure of is that Mrs. Drimley made a decision that morning. The decision was that her old life was over, and her new life had begun. She realized she'd begun to move again when she found herself fingering the scraps of fabric below her hands. She willed movement back into her arms, her toes. She blinked and worked the muscles of her face. She deepened her breaths. She bent her knees.

When Mrs. Drimley sat up and looked around soberly, it was with a face she would not have recognized. Something of the child she'd been, something of the cocooned wife she'd been, and something new, something that set her face to stone and made her movements more forceful.

Mrs. Drimley had a plan, or at least the beginnings of one.

Something from Nothing

Mulligan had been sobered when the door had been slammed in his face the previous night. He'd sat and worried over Mrs. Drimley for a bit, then he'd taken a look around at all the fabric he'd strewn around the house. Perhaps he had gotten a bit carried away. He'd spent the night gathering all the bits of cloth from around the house, and piling them nicely in the second floor hall. All the bits he could reach, that is. How had that strip of cloth landed up on the hanging pot? He'd never know. Once he'd gathered all there was to gather, he curled up in front of Mrs. Drimley's door and settled in for a nap.

When Mrs. Drimley found him there the following morning, she'd nudged him gently with her toes.

"Wake up, Mulligan," she said, "and bring all of that cloth in here. We have work to do."

Mulligan rolled slowly, like melting butter, exposing his belly fluff. He twisted this way and that, thoroughly

enjoying his morning stretch. Mrs. Drimley wasn't having it, though. She knew this could go on for hours.

"Mulligan, get moving."

"What's the rush, Mrs. Drimley? What do you intend to do with all these...leftovers." Mulligan treaded carefully and lightly with his words. He'd not left a single piece of uncut fabric in the entire collection.

"Mulligan. I am in no state of mind to have a conversation about this with you. You have all but destroyed what I have been keeping for decades. Do not trifle with me. Just do as I say," Mrs. Drimley ordered through gritted teeth.

Mulligan gulped. He began moving the fabric beside the table where Mrs. Drimley pointed, but with little gusto. You would think Mulligan would feel some sense of responsibility for Mrs. Drimley's current mood. Instead, he entertained notions of having been slighted and treated unfairly. He'd gathered the scraps from around the house, hadn't he? In his mind that act of repentance had more than made up for the original offence. Mulligan simply was not an individual inclined to recognize the full implications of his actions any more than Mrs. Drimley was inclined to acknowledge his sulking.

She immediately set about laying pieces out on her workspace. She arranged the scraps on the table exchanging this piece for that piece until she was satisfied. Then she sat at her sewing machine and stitched the pieces out just

as she had laid them out on the table. It was like a puzzle. The only goals were to create a square, and to waste as little of Mrs. Drimley's precious fabric as possible.

Mrs. Drimley made squares that looked like rainbows. She made squares that looked like fire. Some were the color of the sea. Shades of bold green made a blanket of grass. Bright pinks and yellows became a field of flowers. Every square was different. Every square was beautiful. Mulligan did her bidding, working as her assistant all day. "Hand me that piece, Mulligan," was the extent of their conversation all day long.

Mulligan's sulky attitude began to melt as the pieces came together. They were grand. He nearly told Mrs. Drimley so, but the sharpness of her eyes kept him from speaking. There are times when silence really is golden.

Mrs. Drimley worked with determined focus. She worked through the puzzle of each square, noting how the patterns in the fabric complimented or clashed against each other. With her eyes full of the spectrum of color, her mind was full of the dull grayness of the market and the bland fear and anger that radiated from the eyes she met there. She could not begin to understand why Mr. Drimley had made up stories of a thriving market rather than tell her the truth about the place he sold fish every day. Where was the sense in that?

Mrs. Drimley also couldn't make sense of Florie. How could someone with so much, who was so much,

hide away from the world? Whatever little tricks she was weaving, Mrs. Drimley thought that somehow she could have used those tricks to brighten the market, not add to its grayness. Mr. Appleton was clearly at the bottom of the whole strange world. Certainly he was large enough to intimidate all the others, but a man afraid of the woods couldn't be too much of a threat, could he?

All she knew for sure was that she was going back. She was going to speak to her sister. And she was going to have a market stand of her own. A market stand that was not the slightest bit bland...

What Mr. Appleton Thinks

Mr. Frederick Appleton admired his reflection in the mirror. His chest heaved with determined satisfaction. One by one, Mr. Appleton fastened the black buttons on his grey vest. There was nothing tattered about his clothes. And rightly so. It had taken years for his ridiculous wife to make a satisfactory garment. He'd been carried away by her beauty, by the way her eyes only looked at the ground below his feet. How stupid of him not to know that she'd be worthless and without skill.

He and his mother had taken care of that. God rest her soul. What would he have done without his mother during those early years? She, who knew what he deserved: a wife to serve him. In the end, even when she was prop-erly trained, when his mother's cold body had been laid deep below the grassy earth, a capable wife had not been enough.

He'd used what he learned from bettering his wife to train this whole settlement of people to serve him well. Now they all knew to look down when he was coming.

They all knew what they owed him. It took some time, but he'd done it. All you really need to do is care for a person in a moment of weakness, then, if you manage yourself intelligently, you are free to lord over them forever. And of course, they were better off for his guidance and help. Before he'd organized the market, people had wandered the countryside, spending days traveling from one house to another to trade goods and labor. Because of him, Appleton had become an official settlement. Because of him, a post office had been brought. As he stared at his reflection, he saw the city of Appleton growing vast in his eyes. It would all be his.

His mother had taken him and moved toward the sea, fleeing her own, very real monster, when Mr. Appleton was but a small child. She'd described the perilous journey to him as he grew, telling him of how the monster's shadow had seemed to follow them through the forest. She'd told him that their only hope for happiness was here, away from the woods, since the shadow could still be hovering there waiting to catch them at its very first chance. All they had to do was stay out of the darkness of the woods to survive.

And he did survive. He thrived even. He grew into a fine, strong boy, devoted to his mother's happiness. He grew into her protector and provider. For her, he had cleared land, removing one tree at a time, creating a wider and wider circle of protection from the shadows she feared; the shadows he hated with all his might. And yet,

he couldn't help but resent her constant watching. On a stump, she would sit with her knitting needles working yet another sweater, but her eyes never left him.

As a young man, he put all of his anger into the swing of an axe. He imagined bringing down the shadow, even if it meant removing every tree in sight. To this very day, he continued to take down a tree daily. He was careful not to step foot into the shadow, even as his heart raged. He'd thought many times of going in to face the shadow. Many times he had proposed to do just that. His mother had fretted, begged, ordered and threatened, and when that hadn't worked, she'd cried. This consistently brought him to his knees asking for her forgiveness.

The first time he'd struck his wife, he'd found her in the woods with their first child, a child his mother had said was born under an unlucky star. He was appalled at his wife's failure to attend to their child's safety. He'd drug her from the woods and struck her down with the baby still in her arms. He'd watched her few tears dampen the ground as she clutched the baby to her chest. His resolve flinched, but he stiffened his spine. She would simply have to learn to stay out of the woods now, just as he had. She hadn't gone into the woods again, but there was always something. Soon he found that every day a burst of anger ended with a bit of her blood on his knuckles. This, he knew, was the price of marrying an inferior woman. If only she would listen and learn.

The children she bore were like her. It would take a lifetime to train a boy to be fit for taking over his city when it was time for him to join his mother in the ground. If she'd ever have one that was worthy of the task, it would surely be a weight off his mind. As it stood, he was the only person within the settlement that had the skills to organize and help everyone manage their affairs. It was the kind of burden only a selfless man would take on.

Mr. Appleton straightened his vest and pulled on his jacket with a sigh. His neck tightened at the sound of a baby's cry. He strode down the hall toward the door, thrusting one of the children to the side as he passed. Honestly. Could she not teach them the simple respect of stepping aside when their father was walking by?

Going Back

It took several trips up and down the cliff to load all the materials Mrs. Drimley had prepared for the market into the little rowboat. Mrs. Drimley forcefully blocked all the images of the waves and capsizing boats and goods floating helplessly to rest on the sand below that crept into her mind. She would not admit to worry, but Mrs. Drimley had been undeniably anxious for days. She was sharp with Mulligan, and all but transfixed by her work. She did not share her plans with Mulligan at this time.

He'd stayed close to her and had watched as closely as he had through the months of silent knitting last fall. Mrs. Drimley did have the tendency to sink into her thoughts when she was troubled, and this troubled Mulligan. He wished she would at least tell him what she was thinking. As it was, he was completely clueless, something Mulligan was not a bit fond of. For example, he had no idea what had happened during her first trip to the market. He did not even know if this change in

mannerisms was from his thoughtless use of her goods or something more.

Mulligan had been dedicated in his assistance. Once she saw that he could sew straight lines, she allowed him to do much of the sewing. She did notice the joy it brought him, and she was not angry enough to want to keep him miserable.

Once she'd secured all of the market goods in the boat she called up to Mulligan, "I'll be back before sundown, Mulligan! Try not to destroy the house this time."

Mulligan nodded his agreement, and made his way back to the house. It had only been a week since Mrs. Drimley's first trip to the market, but he felt himself to be a much older cat. His walk was more dignified, he thought, made even more so by the silk lavender vest he'd chosen for the day. He still held out hope for a top hat. This week had not seemed the right time to ask for assistance from Mrs. Drimley to design fashionable catwear, what with all the flurry of salvaging the scraps he'd made. At any rate, he was determined to use his day as a dignified cat would.

As Mulligan was settling onto his lately neglected cushion, and preparing his mind for great cat thoughts between snoozes, Mrs. Drimley was navigating her way toward the market dock. It was much windier today. The little boat held strong, rising and falling with the swells.

Mrs. Drimley was relieved by the need for absolute concentration. Overthinking her choices would not do. Brooding over them would be even worse, so she focused

all her energy on getting to the dock in one piece with all her goods still in tow.

This time, she anticipated the dock keeper, and had prepared herself to request and receive his help. Certainly, that should be the easiest part of the day.

Mrs. Drimley managed to stop at the dock without sliding underneath it this time around. The dock keeper good naturedly took the packages, all wrapped in home-spun cloth, from her and piled them on the dock.

"Good day for a trip to market, Mrs. Drimley. A might bit windy, though. I see you fared well."

Mrs. Drimley was taken by surprise when he'd called her by name. No doubt, it took no time at all for word to travel in a small place like this.

"It took all my strength to stay on course, but I've made it," Mrs. Drimley replied.

"I see you have," the dock keeper said with a crass smile as he looked Mrs. Drimley up and down in wonder.

Mrs. Drimley cleared her throat forcefully. "Sir. You know my name, but I do not know yours."

"Eh. Name's Morville," he replied absently while staring unabashedly at her lower half.

You see, Mrs. Drimley had donned a pair of Mr. Drimley's work pants that morning. The idea of wandering around the market, or up and down the cliff for that matter, with a tied up skirt again did not sound like a winning idea to Mrs. Drimley. A pair of pants, however,

was just the thing, and she knew just where to find them. Thank goodness she hadn't cut them up with the shirts!

She picked a dark pair of thick brown woolen pants. They were a bit too large around the middle, but one of her skirt belts had fixed that without a problem. Mrs. Drimley thought they were just wonderful. She'd tucked one of her button up tops into them and had wrapped her pink scarf thrice around her neck before tying it around her middle as a makeshift sweater vest. Yes, she had thought, that would do very well.

Mr. Morville stood on the dock staring freely at her, still, wondering where on God's green earth this woman had come from.

Mrs. Drimley audibly sighed at the man's rudeness, "If you could please help me with these packages, Mr. Morville, I'd be appreciative."

Mr. Morville shook his head as though he were waking himself. "Couldn't leave the dock, ma'am, but I can loan you the use of this cart."

Mrs. Drimley eyed the shabby cart with its wobbly wooden wheel skeptically, then thought to herself, *if the boat works, certainly this will, too.* Then she replied to Mr. Morville, "Thank you. That will be helpful."

Mr. Morville helped Mrs. Drimley load her packages into the cart and was shaking his head as he watched her manage the heavy cart on the path through the woods.

The Drimley Space

Mrs. Drimley tried to look respectable pushing the jalopy of a cart along the uneven path. She heaved the rickety wheel over rocks and through divots with quiet determination.

Her arms shook with the effort of heaving the heavy cart forward, and with anticipation of setting out her goods. She had no idea if anyone would purchase them in the market, and she cared little. She had an indescribable confidence that these goods would be a way for her to earn money. Her plan was to talk to Florie about the goods if they did not raise any interest in the market.

As she stepped out into the light of the market, she did so quietly. She hoped to set up her goods undisturbed, and without drawing attention to herself. While no one approached her as she unwrapped her goods, she could feel the eyes peering at her back the minute she began to make use of the stand marked Drimley. It still stank of fish even after the seasons that had passed since any

fish had touched the stand. Mrs. Drimley made a mental note to order a can of paint after she'd made a sale or two, which might suffocate the smell and liven up the stand.

Mrs. Drimley had mostly made cushion covers and pieced blankets. But she had used some of the more subtle fabrics to piece a vest, and all the pinks she had sewn into a full skirt. After she'd arranged her goods, she paced around to the back of the market stand. It felt peculiar, standing there waiting for someone to show an interest in what she'd made. She lasted only a moment before she paced to the edge of the woods to gather wildflowers. The stench of her stand was overwhelming. She grabbed an armful of flowers, then made her way back to her stand. With the flowers laying prettily along the back of her stand, Mrs. Drimley arranged herself so that her nose was positioned directly on top of the flowers. It helped with the fishy odor, but it did not solve it.

Mrs. Drimley was practicing the art of breathing discreetly through her mouth when a child wandered up to her stand. He was filthy from head to toe. She recognized him immediately as one of her nephews.

"Hello," she greeted him with a straight face, though her heart was pounding in her chest. He looked just like her father must have looked when he was a child, dark eyed, round cheeked, plump in the arms and legs, curly topped. He stared at her openly. His eyes and face held

no expression, but Mrs. Drimley could feel his expression beneath the surface wanting to peak out. Is this what Mr. Drimley had seen when he met her in the woods that day? The boy, his eyes never leaving her face, reached a grubby finger up slowly and petted the pink skirt, which had been draped over the front of the stand. Then, eyes still planted on her, he sunk his nose into the skirt and inhaled deeply. Mrs. Drimley shuddered a bit at that, because his nose was both smudged with soil and crusted around the nostrils. She tried not to show her concern. The boy opened his mouth to speak when suddenly his arm was jerked forcefully from behind.

Mrs. Drimley took in the sight of her sister with the baby in her arms, a fresh bruise swelling on her cheek bone, and the boy cowering below his mother's grip.

He only whimpered when his mother's hand went up, but he stood to take what he knew was coming. "You don't run from me," she hissed through clenched teeth.

"No. Stop!" Mrs. Drimley shouted.

Mrs. Appleton turned a cloudy eye toward her sister and brewed a storm with her stare. Mrs. Drimley nearly silenced herself under the hatred in her sister's eyes, but the image of the boy's soft caress on the pink skirt was too fresh in her mind.

"What's happened to you?"

"What did you ever know of me? And what do you care of us?"

"I never knew anything of you but torment. Things can be different, Angeline."

There was a moment that passed with their eyes locked in a silent test of wills. They were well matched, which must have come as a shock to Mrs. Appleton, who only ever thought of her sister Elsa as the dullard who'd struggled as much to meet someone's eye as she did with the buckets of water she'd been made to carry.

I must explain, at this moment, that Mrs. Appleton managed to keep her dignity by treating everyone around her with the same severity as her husband showed her. She was under him, but everyone else was under her. That was the way her world was supposed to work. It was a bargain she made with herself every time he laid his hands or fists or feet on her. It was how she carried on, and it usually pleased her to see him lord over others. So, when she walked slowly to her sister's market stand and laid out this warning, it was done with cold love.

"Elsa Dora, you ought to go back to where you came from and take these frills with you. My husband is no man to trifle with. You've no idea what he's capable of."

"I can see for myself what he's capable of," Mrs. Drimley replied pointedly, allowing her gaze to rest on her sister's swollen cheek.

Mrs. Appleton threw back her shoulders and said with a sneer, "Don't feel sorry for me." Then she turned to walk home, her children lining up behind her, heads

bowed. The boy who'd run away tried to jerk away from his mother's grip and reached for Mrs. Drimley, whose eyes were brimmed fully with tears. Mrs. Appleton gave the boy's arm a firm jerk and stopped abruptly, leaning down to be level with his face. "Your father will beat us both senseless and it is your fault."

Mrs. Drimley wanted to go wrestle the boy out of her sister's arms. Her whole body quaked with outrage and sadness, but what could she do? She had no right to take the boy. She steeled her feet to the ground and promised in her heart that she'd do something, no matter how long it took. She must have promised loudly, because the boy turned his head for a moment. Where there was once only a blank expression, Mrs. Drimley saw something, and it looked like hope.

Mulligan Cooks

Mrs. Drimley had sold nothing that day. She tried telling herself that discouragement shouldn't be her response since she hadn't expected to sell anything. Only the tiny boy had been brave enough to even approach the table. She wondered, should she go back tomorrow? Then there was Florie. When she'd gone to see if her package arrived, she'd gone knowing that anything could happen. She was braced for the unusual, but what she found there was not only the usual, but the mundane. Florie had said only, "Come back tomorrow and check again," gruffly, and then turned back to her shuffling and sorting.

Tomorrow! Mrs. Drimley could hardly think of coming back the next day. She was exhausted. She'd only planned on a weekly trip to the market. Surely that was often enough.

As she had the week before, Mrs. Drimley used the time rowing to let off steam. The feelings came right out of her heart, flowed down her arms and powered the rows mightily. She was tying up the boat in no time. She found

a cavernous space at the bottom of the cliff to keep her goods for the night. No sense in carrying them up and down if she'd be going back tomorrow. In her pants, she was up the cliff in a flash. In fact, going up and down the cliff felt entirely normal now. Was it just the week before that she'd been so terrified at the prospect? She was weary, though, and she looked forward to having a hot bowl of anything and putting her feet up for the night.

She could smell the food before she got to the door. How could that be? She was expecting only to find fish waiting to be cooked. But no, the aroma of a warm, hearty meal was tickling her senses. She opened the door to the kitchen almost cautiously, not knowing what she'd find, but there, in a spotless kitchen was Mulligan standing on his hind legs on a stool in a lavender vest stirring a bubbling pot.

Mulligan had discovered that afternoon that he enjoyed himself in front of the stove nearly as much as he did behind the sewing machine. Once he mastered the use of the knife, and how to lean over the pot without singeing his fur, he found the process of cooking extremely creative and satisfying.

Mrs. Drimley's mouth dropped open. There was a brief moment during which she considered the cleanliness of a cat in the kitchen, but the delicious smells chased the questions out of her mind.

Mulligan turned, delighted to see Mrs. Drimley as she

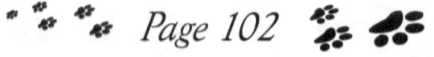

collapsed into the nearest chair. He had a bowl of soup in front of her in a flash.

"I'm so glad you're home. It was positively silent all day long. I'm dying to talk to someone. Have you ever tasted such delectable soup? I guarantee you haven't, what with all that horrid stew you ate for all those years." Mulligan literally bit his tongue. *Kindness,* he thought to himself as he studied Mrs. Drimley. Clearly she'd had a trying day. "Tell me, did you sell anything at the market? Has my eyepiece come?"

Mrs. Drimley's shoulders felt like they were carrying one hundred pounds each. She slumped over the soup and dipped her spoon gradually into her soup, inhaling deeply. It did smell divine. "My day was heart sickening," she honestly replied. "Nothing sold, and your eyepiece did not come, though Florie said I should check again tomorrow. Tomorrow," she repeated.

Mulligan cleared his throat and watched for her to take her first bite of soup. She took her time about it. Mulligan was practically leaning over Mrs. Drimley's bowl by the time the soup touched her lips. The tense lines in her face softened and her eyes brightened considerably. *Ahh,* Mulligan sat back, satisfied, and complimented himself on a job well done.

"Nothing treats heart sickness like a bowl of soup." Mulligan sagely exhaled.

Mrs. Drimley studied her cat leaning back with his head

resting back luxuriously on furry paws. Fluff was bursting out of the fitted vest he wore around his two front legs. She was, as she had been since the day he'd first spoken, really since the day he'd showed up as a tiny kitten with three fish bigger than himself, completely bewildered. She thought herself to be approaching, if not arriving at, her right mind. Her right mind, however, could not make sense of this talking, cooking, sewing cat.

She sat, sipping–slurping, if I'm going to be honest— the most delicious soup she'd ever tasted wondering if what had actually happened when Mr. Drimley died was that she'd lost her mind. That would explain the cooking cat. It would also explain why she'd thought the post lady was magical...

"Yes, I do wonder about her, myself," Mulligan said aloud.

Mrs. Drimley jumped in her seat. She'd been deeply lost in her thoughts. "What did you say?" she questioned skeptically.

"I said I do wonder about her. Florie," Mulligan said the name as though it gave him a sour taste in his mouth.

"How did you know I was thinking about Florie?" Mrs. Drimley questioned.

"Oh, were you thinking? I don't mean to reply to your thoughts. You were thinking loudly. You do that, you know," Mulligan said nonchalantly as he filled a bowl for his own supper.

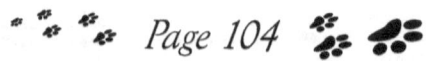

Mulligan sat his bowl down then nobly began to lap his soup.

"For heaven's sake, Mulligan," Mrs. Drimley said dryly, "don't lap your food at the dinner table."

Mulligan glanced up at her with comical irritation. "Really, woman. You really are going mad. I am what I am."

"Why can you stir with a spoon, but not eat with one?" Mrs. Drimley demanded.

"Why does it matter?" Mulligan retorted, then went back to his lapping.

"Because you don't make sense! None of this makes any sense!" Mrs. Drimley emphatically declared.

"My good lady, it's a wonder you've made it this far into your life thinking that everything should make sense." Mulligan sniffed haughtily into his soup while Mrs. Drimley narrowed her eyes at him.

"Do you know what happened at the market today?"

"How should I know what happened at the market today? I've been here all day long."

"Well, you seem to know things you shouldn't. Like, what I'm thinking, for example."

"What, you think I'm psychic? A psychic cat? How ridiculous."

"You *are* ridiculous. You're a cat! In a vest! A vest you sewed! Eating soup you cooked! That *is* ridiculousness!" Mrs. Drimley was getting hysterical.

"Settle down, lady, you'll make yourself ill. If you want

me to explain myself, I'm going to disappoint you, because I can't. How am I to know why I am what I am?"

Mrs. Drimley stared at Mulligan lapping comfortably, as though they'd been talking about the weather, which looked to be brewing into a storm. As she stared, a thought began to form. Mrs. Drimley realized that what she felt when she looked at Mulligan was envy: envy at his ease with himself, his confidence. As soon as she realized this, her insides began to replicate the outside weather. A storm was brewing. She quietly ate her soup and stared out the window.

Mulligan's Desire

The storm lasted for three days. Mrs. Drimley grew listless. She worried about the packages she'd left by the shore. She could not focus on making any new goods or on cooking or cleaning. She only felt dissatisfication with her feelings, her reflection, her creations, the cat, her interactions with her sister. Many times a day the image of the sweet boy flooded her mind, stealing her breath and her composure. Her heart willed kindness to be wrapped around that child, but she knew it was imaginary. Willing protection was just her way of resolving her panic—she felt helpless, and it was nearly unbearable.

Mulligan went about his business. Truly, he took care of all her needs during those stormy days. Mrs. Drimley thanked him for all his actions, but now that she'd recognized the envy she felt, it was hard to be jovial with him. Mulligan did not seem to mind.

Mulligan had grown accustomed to Mrs. Drimley's moods. Fortunately, they seemed to seesaw with his own.

When one was up, the other was down, which worked quite well, really. He had his own plan brewing, which he knew would require careful execution to realize. As much as Mulligan had enjoyed the two days he'd spent at home alone, and as much as he acknowledged his own domestic prowess, he knew that the days of fun would soon turn to days of drudgery. Mulligan wanted to get out. He wanted to see the market. He only needed to find a way to get Mrs. Drimley to take him with her.

He'd briefly considered simply sneaking into the boat, but he sensed that this would do no good for his friendship with Mrs. Drimley. No, he was going to have to get to the market honestly.

On the morning of the third day of the storm, Mrs. Drimley was especially distracted at the breakfast table. Mulligan felt the time was right, so he dove right in.

"You know, I believe my curiosity about the marketplace is getting the better of me, Mrs. Drimley. You've said so little about it."

"What would you like to know?"

"Oh, what it smells like. What the people look like. What color of green is the grass? Who's the friendliest? Who's the most horrible? And I feel nearly desperate to meet this Florie."

Mrs. Drimley raised an eyebrow in Mulligan's direction, then continued to eat.

Mulligan pushed his food around his plate, then said

with forced confidence, "I think there could be a way I could see it all."

"No, Mulligan."

"No, what? You haven't even heard my idea."

"No, you can't go to the market and pretend to be an ordinary cat. You couldn't possibly make it through the day without speaking, and then what? I'm trying to work my way into this town. A talking cat would make me a social pariah!"

Mulligan bristled at that, "A social pariah! How many other women wear pants and row themselves to market? I think you're already a social pariah. I don't see how I could make it worse for you, even if you are right."

Then Mulligan grew sly, "Besides, who knows what I'd get up to at home." Mulligan stared pointedly at Mrs. Drimley, who rolled her eyes and sat down her fork.

"How do I know you'll stay quiet all day. You'll be at great risk if you don't, you know."

"Of course I know. I may be isolated, but I know I'm a rarity. A rare gem of a being."

"Mulligan, please. You have to take this seriously. I need a promise I can believe in."

Mulligan mulled it over. "Well, I won't say I'm not insulted by your lack of trust, but I'll tell you this. If I do not remain quiet for the duration of the day at the market, I will give up wearing vests for a month." Mulligan flung himself back into the chair. This would be no

easy bargain, but if he failed, he thought it a cruel fate.

"Fine. You must look entirely ordinary, Mulligan. That means no vest or scarf or hat on the day of the trip to the market."

"But!" Mulligan leapt back to the table.

Mrs. Drimley gave no sign of recognition to his resistance, in spite of the tragic look on his face.

"Fine. It should be easy to remain silent. I'll be too depressed to make a peep. On the next good day, then."

"Fine."

Mulligan woke up early the next day and peeked out the window. Muggy and misty, but no rain. That was a good sign. They needed only a good wind or a strong stream of sunlight to clear away the fog. Mulligan pranced quietly along the hallway in front of Mrs. Drimley's door. His furry paws didn't make a sound, but his excitement nearly escaped in yips. He clamped his mouth shut and let his feet do the yipping. He was so lost in his dance that he didn't notice when Mrs. Drimley opened the door behind him. His dance slowed as he shifted around and saw Mrs. Drimley standing with her hands on her hips and her eyes raised, one slippered foot peeking out from below the hemline of her nightgown. Mulligan smiled his cattiest smile and said, "No rain."

"Yes, but lots of clouds. On the ground," was Mrs. Drimley's stolid reply.

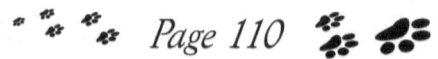

"Oh, those are going to clear right up," Mulligan declared.

"They are, are they?" Mrs. Drimley glanced out the window which was shrouded in thick mist. "I think it's an oatmeal day."

Mulligan hated oatmeal. "I'll just go catch some fish."

"Suit yourself."

Mulligan glumly set out through the fog. He really had no intentions of catching fish this morning. In fact, the whole ordeal of catching fish was beginning to disgust him. He'd been working up the nerve to request that Mrs. Drimley begin keeping chickens, but with the eyepiece purchase being so recent, he really felt it wasn't the best time to propose another expense.

He slunk his way down the path anyway, just in case Mrs. Drimley was watching him. It wouldn't hurt her to feel a little guilty. As he watched the sun burn holes through the clouds, he knew he was right about the day's weather. It would soon be clear enough to embark on their journey. Mulligan's walk grew a little jauntier. He couldn't help but perk up, in spite of his rumbling stomach. He was going to the market. He didn't know why, but he felt destined to be there that day. Something special was going to happen, he just knew it.

Mulligan sauntered around the house, peering into the woods, where he'd not yet explored, what with his preference for cushion sitting over prowling. Besides, his time outdoors was occupied with catching ghastly fish. It

didn't take long before Mulligan was prancing through sunshine rather than slinking through thick dampness. Mulligan had just made his mind up to sneak into the kitchen for a bite, find Mrs. Drimley, and demand that it was time to go when out the lady came with the basket strapped to her shoulders.

She gave him a pointed look that clearly said, "Don't say a word and we'll make our peace," and Mulligan was happy enough to silently follow her. He tried to keep his frolicking to a minimum since she was clearly still out of sorts. But it was hard. He had an appointment with his future life at the market today.

They made their way silently down the cliff and to the shore where Mulligan was more impressed with his Mrs. Drimley's strength than ever. Watching her handle the boat from a distance, where she and the boat looked like tiny toy pieces, was much different than seeing Mrs. Drimley's strain and determination up close. What an ability, to turn over a boat! Mulligan knew he was an extraordinary cat, but it was just now dawning on him that Mrs. Drimley, too, might be extraordinary. He pondered all of this quietly as she rowed their way toward the market. The closer they got, the more miserable Mrs. Drimley looked, and the more difficult it was for Mulligan to restrain his excitement. Oh, yes. Mulligan just knew he was about to meet his destiny.

To Market, To Market to Meet the Fat Pig

Mulligan sat immovable on the path at the edge of the wood. Mrs. Drimley had, again, borrowed the cart from the dock manager and was struggling through the bumpy grass toward the Drimley market stand. Mulligan was sobered, to say the very least; disgusted, to be more accurate. He attempted to swallow his disappointment. He tried to lift his paw to move toward the stand when Mrs. Drimley motioned for him to come along, but he found he was frozen on the path. Mrs. Drimley shook her head and set about arranging her items, in vain, she was sure. Even so, she was determined to be here at least once a week, if only to make a point.

More than anything, she was eager to get to the post office, but it felt important to take her place at the stand. This is what people were meant to do to make a living, and what else was there for her to do, but find some way to make money to live on? Being here meant she was not giving up. It meant she knew she could do

for herself what Mr. Drimley had done for them both.

Mrs. Drimley heard the Appletons arriving before she saw them. Mr. Appleton was along today. It was his voice that rang venomously over the market path toward them. The words echoed together so that they were indiscernible, but the tone was easy enough to interpret. Mrs. Drimley thought of the children who must be trailing after that odious man and set her mouth in a line of stone.

Mulligan, having heard the unsettling voice, had been stirred from his rigidity and had made his way to Mrs. Drimley's side. The stand still reeked of fish, and Mulligan's cat nature and refined habits were doing inner battle. It's a strange experience to be recoiled and enticed all at the same time. He found his balance by sitting calmly on the stand. From there, he had a fantastic view of the underwhelming market, for which he could think of only one descriptive word. Bland.

Mrs. Drimley whispered a warning to Mulligan as the Appletons made their way around the market stands. Mr. Appleton seemed to be collecting money from the people there, who looked deflated once the stream of Appletons had passed them by. "Don't forget your promise Mulligan. You're just a simple cat."

"May I meow?" Mulligan slyly requested with simpering eyes. Mrs. Drimley smiled in spite of herself.

All at once the Appletons were upon them. Mrs. Apple-

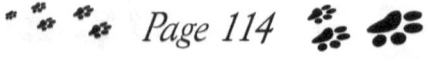

ton's eyes seemed to be glued to the ground, while Mr. Appleton allowed his eyes to convey their revulsion all over Mrs. Drimley's goods. It began to feel as though he were going to stand there all day casting his judgement, so for the good of all present, Mrs. Drimley broke the silence.

"Sir?" she stated.

Mr. Appleton roughly cleared his throat with a derisive ahem. "Madam." He grinned, though his body seemed to be rocking and puffing up. "What is this you're attempting to sell in my market?"

"Home goods," Mrs. Drimley replied dryly.

"Not very respectable, though. Where have you found... no, never mind. Well, you must know that having a stand here at the market comes with its price, and you'll pay it now." He stepped closer, seeming to grow taller as he made this demand.

Mrs. Drimley thought fast. She'd not earned any money at the market, and she was nearly out of cash.

"Sir, has this not been the Drimley stand for years? That's what I have been told. And did Mr. Drimley not set the stand on this side of the field, away from all the others expressly to avoid being on your ground? As this ground is more adjacent to the post office ground, I would think that this land is not your property, but the property of the government." Mrs. Drimley was attempting to keep her quaking inside of her skin and out of the vision of Mr. Appleton. She had no clue if what she said was true or not. She had no idea where these

ideas were even coming from; they were practically out of her mouth before she'd thought them up. Even so, they seemed to have an effect on Mr. Appleton.

"You Drimleys," said Mr. Appleton through a gritted smile. Then he laughed in a stiffed, choked way that made Mulligan wonder if he had a hairball. Mrs. Drimley saw Mrs. Appleton's eyes slide up without any movement of her head. Mrs. Drimley held that glance as long as she could. Something had changed in those eyes. Instead of screaming with hatred, those eyes were saying help.

"You know, Mr. Appleton. If I were you, I'd think about treating people a little nicer. If all these people realized all at one time that you were just a person, you could have a riot on your hands."

Mr. Appleton scoffed openly at Mrs. Drimley then grew very still. "That sounded like a threat, Mrs. Drimley. I hope it wasn't, because I have neither the time nor the patience for people who don't fall in line."

"What a shame I'm not afraid of you, then, Mr. Appleton. It must be so inconvenient to have your patience tried." Mrs. Drimley did not know where all this spunk was coming from. She was scared down to her bones, but she'd eat dirt before letting him see it. She'd been safe and loved for far too long to slip back into a role of subservience.

"You will be." Mr. Appleton's voice had turned to gravel. As he turned to leave, he struck his wife's head with his open hand. She didn't flinch, but Mrs. Drimley leapt

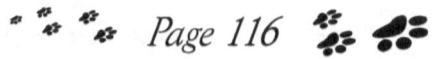

and clung to her stand for strength. Angeline looked up at her sister, struggling to communicate through her eyes. The time was too short, and Mrs. Drimley was too riled to understand. The wail in her throat was strangled, not able to come out, and as she watched the line of children fall into place, she pounded her fist on her stand. Somewhere deep in her gut she knew that if Mr. Appleton were to find out that she was his wife's sister, it would put Angeline and her children in grave danger.

Just as she had the week before, she wanted to go rip the children away to safety, and now, her sister, too. But she also knew she could not do it yet, and certainly not against Angeline's will. Angeline was following that horrible man for who knows what reason to who knows what end. It made Mrs. Drimley sick to her stomach to think what might happen to her sister and those children in the moments to come. She felt so helpless. Underneath the agony, though, there was a golden thread of hope that said everything was going to work out. She gripped it with all her might.

After the scene at the market, the townspeople kept even more of a distance between themselves and Mrs. Drimley than they had before, if that was possible. Mulligan, however, had been quick to pounce once the Appletons had disappeared from sight.

"What is going on, Madame. You've not spoken a word of this." It was clear now what had been bothering Mrs. Drimley so deeply. And here Mulligan had thought she'd just been working through the kinks of entering life. What a rude welcome she was getting to it.

"I told you it wasn't what you thought it was going to be."

"Well, yes, but that could mean anything! This is so far below my expectations...it could not be worse."

"Don't say that, Mulligan," said Mrs. Drimley, who suddenly was overcome with the desire to not tempt fate.

"Just who is that woman? And don't skirt my question. You know her, but how could you possibly..." Mulligan was rambling.

"She's my sister, Mulligan."

Mulligan, who had clamped his mouth defiantly shut upon being interrupted, now let it fall back open.

"Her name is Angeline. She's four years older than I am, and she left home long before I did. When we were both there, she only paid notice to me when she was giving orders. Frankly, I don't know her at all. There was certainly never any love between us. I'm not sure there was any love in that house at all. In fact I'm sure there wasn't. But...I can't explain it. There's a pull in my bones. "

"Yes, I can feel that. Makes total sense. I still wonder about the other kittens in my litter." Mulligan trailed off, suddenly realizing that he couldn't remember those other kittens.

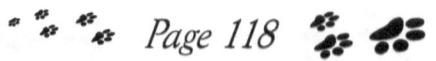

"Well, I never did. I never wondered about any of them. It was as though it all just slipped away once I left. I just assumed that they had all found their ways as well. My father, he probably rotted in that chair." The truth was that Mrs. Drimley had felt next to nothing about her family since the day she'd left, and now, seeing Angeline like this was pricking at her nerves in places she had no desire to be pricked. Luckily, Mrs. Drimley's habit of addressing only what was immediately at hand was well established. It helped her survive. It helped her focus on the matter-of-fact things she had to do.

Mulligan, as we have seen, was not in possession of this habit, and his mind wandered around and around and around the events at the market all morning long. He was still pondering when they reached the post office that he'd been so eager to get to. It no longer seemed urgent to him to get his eyepiece.

A Turning

Mulligan pawed into the post office, barely even considering his eye piece. When Mrs. Drimley asked if her package had arrived, the elderly, unkempt woman behind the counter, whom Mulligan could not see properly, replied that it had come and she went into the storage room to retrieve it. It was then that Mulligan's excitement returned. After all these weeks, there was a chance that his sight might, in fact, clear up again At very least, Mulligan was sure he'd look regal with a smart eye piece. He leapt to the countertop, and stayed there, though Mrs. Drimley urged him to get down.

"Any ordinary cat would do just this," Mulligan whispered to Mrs. Drimley, who rolled her eyes in return.

Mulligan pawed the countertop while he waited; he was so excited he could not possibly sit still. He was about to betray his dignity and flop onto his back, such was his eagerness, when Florie came out with a box wrapped in brown paper. Mulligan eyed Florie sharply. There was

something terribly familiar about her. She, in turn, avoided eye contact with him, but her hand trembled slightly when she laid the package down.

"So, this is the cat the eyepiece is for, is it?" Florie asked, directing her question to Mrs. Drimley.

"Oh, yes," Mrs. Drimley replied, trying to sound nonchalant.

"How is it that you knew the cat was having eye problems?" Florie asked.

"Well, he nearly froze one day, and when he finally thawed out and came to, he said...that is, he *seemed* to have...tenderness in his eye, and the lid droops ever so slightly, you see, so I just thought, perhaps, he might be having a little trouble," Mrs. Drimley quickly rambled.

"Mmm hmmm," Florie replied, dropping the inquiry and changing topics said, "Do you have your goods you came in with last week, by chance?"

"Yes, of course I do."

"Well, I've heard from a shop in one of the southern cities that would love to see your work. This could be an excellent way to bring in extra income, which you need now."

"Here, send it all," Mrs. Drimley replied, absently hoisting her packages from the cart onto the counter. "Clearly it won't be selling in the Appleton market."

"Will do," Florie replied watching Mrs. Drimley closely. "Mr. Appleton's a special case, that one."

Something in this phrase pricked Mulligan's ears, and

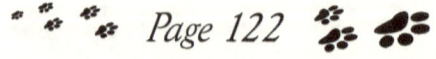

he took a closer look at Florie. From the sticks in her hair to her slouching dirty stockings, Mulligan found her image repulsive. Still, when he looked at her, he smelled flowers. This did not make sense. He wanted desperately to have a conversation with this lady, but he wasn't about to break his promise to Mrs. Drimley. Not now. Not after the day she'd had.

"Yes, well, special isn't the word I'd use to describe him. Especially revolting, perhaps." Mrs. Drimley did not even try to hide her feelings.

"You'll want to be careful, whatever you do, Mrs. Drimley. He's not one to be trifled with, though I'll admit he's done a number on the people of this town," Florie casually replied.

"Oh yes, how so?"

"Well, being here at the post office, I catch wind of people's troubles. Yes, he'll help out a family when they hit a rough patch, but then, he's at their door, hovering, demanding thanks; in the form of servitude, if you ask me. Once you've accepted a favor from that man, he sees to it that you do things his way. Everyone's just plain terrified of him, and for good reason. Many's the family who's lost their home after defying him, even in small ways. Mysterious fires, you see. No proof that it's him. No one to stand against him."

"What have you been doing all this time?" Mrs. Drimley demanded.

"Watching and waiting, dear. Staying out of his way,

for the most part," Florie replied with real sadness, even regret in her voice.

Mrs. Drimley was seeing clearly why Florie had gone to such lengths to appear as she did, why she had dug that tunnel...had that day been real? If her brief experience was any measurement, staying out of Mr. Appleton's way took a great deal of effort. Then it dawned on her.

"What about Mr. Drimley? He never spoke a word of any of this to me. If he were here, I wouldn't know whether to thank him or give him a stern talking to."

"I quite agree," Florie replied, "I had thought, myself, that...well...all that's over now."

"Just how well did you know my husband, Florie?"

"We were friends. Good friends. He was here daily. After he'd sold his fish at the market, he'd bring packages in to ship out. Orders, you know. Of his woodworking. Stunk something awful. Simply reeked of fish. But what beautiful pieces he made."

Mrs. Drimley thought of her home, built by her husband, and furnished by him, too. Yes, he did beautiful work. She wasn't surprised that people had wanted to purchase his work. She was only surprised by her lack of interest. She'd never wondered at all what he'd done in his workshop.

"He traded for trinkets, he did. Fabric, thread, yarn. He tucked the packages deep into that basket there before he traipsed back to his boat. He'd learned the coarse art of living widely around Mr. Appleton, too."

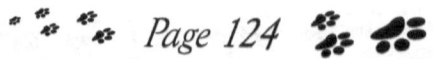

"Yes."

Mrs. Drimley stood there imagining Mr. Drimley in the workshop she'd never stepped foot in, building and carving beautiful shelves and trinkets. She imagined him wrapping carefully the goods that came in return. She remembered the twinkle in his eyes as he watched her open yet another package of treasures.

It never seemed terribly important. Pure expressions of love rarely seem to be grand. They are often quiet. A noticing. A joy that is felt on your behalf. They are actions that whisper *I am paying attention to what brings you happiness and peace.*

A tear formed in the corner of Mrs. Drimley's eye. It is a cruel fate to only realize how pure a love was after it has passed. The beauty in sad endings is that once something is over, there is no chance of soiling it. The love is frozen in time, to be kept deep in the heart, and drawn upon on a hollow night or a shattering day. Mrs. Drimley tucked an unsoilable love into her heart at that very moment. And something happens when you have that kind of love in your heart. I cannot explain it, but it's the reason that Mrs. Drimley discovered her next great purpose, and it's the place she drew her bravery from in the days to come.

Part III

How it Ends

Mr. Appleton Faces the Woods

Mr. Appleton stood in the dense fog at the edge of the woods considering his options. The path was grown over from lack of use. It had been used infrequently even before the odious Drimley man had passed. Mr. Appleton had watched him come out of the woods using the well-hidden path on occasion. This was rare, of course, because the fisherman had come daily to port with his small boat laden heavily with fish to sell. Mr. Appleton scoffed at the memory. The man had practically given those fish away.

There had been something deeply troubling about that man. He smiled too much. He feared too little. He never once showed a hint of subservience to Mr. Appleton, and never had he required assistance, much to Mr. Appleton's dismay. Even when he'd threatened the townspeople not to purchase fish from this man, he still came consistently,

bringing a load of fish to the market. No amount of sly threats or stories swayed him. He laughed when Mr. Appleton had threatened to set fire to his home, and said, "Oh, but sir, my home is deep in the *woods*," with a wink and a superior smile on his face. "You wouldn't want to venture through the *shadows*, would you, now?" Then he'd laughed more, and Mr. Appleton had backed away, threatening him to just keep his mouth shut about woods and shadows and maybe, just maybe, Mr. Drimley would get to keep his house.

He'd done nothing, though he'd seen the path, and when Mr. Drimley quit appearing at the market, Mr. Appleton believed his one bump in the road to full power had leveled out. But here, now, was this woman, of all things, and he could not stand for her insubordination: her lack of fear. She would not be easily controlled, he could see this. He simply needed to take care of her, something he should have done long ago with her husband. The sun was beginning to beam through the surrounding clouds. Soon there would be at least a bit more light along the path.

"Sorry Mother," he mumbled, and then began swinging his ax.

A Plan and A Pattern

"My dear Mrs. Drimley, I believe I see a face in the woods!" Mulligan had frozen mid-grooming on the windowsill when he'd seen a flash in the woods, then had half shrieked before yelling his announcement.

"What in the world are you hollering about? Have you eaten yet today, Mulligan? I know you're much beyond the fish innards now, but the heel of the bread is still left on the table." Mrs. Drimley bellowed from her workroom, clearly with pins between her teeth. She was working on more cushions to send away for sale.

"Of course I've eaten. I haven't gone mad. Come watch for yourself. Someone is lurking out there."

Mrs. Drimley came grudgingly down the stairs and stalked to the window, bending to look from Mulligan's perspective. She gave it a full thirty seconds before turning with a huff. "Mulligan, I think you need to get out more."

"No! There! Bah, you missed it. Just come and look awhile. He looks half mad!"

 *Page 131*

Mrs. Drimley rolled her eyes and took a steadying breath. She heaved a chair up to the window and sat dutifully behind Mulligan, watching for she knew not what. Until she, too, caught a glimmer in the woods.

"What was that?" she said, startled, in spite of herself. "Just a squirrel, surely."

"No. Keep watching."

"Oh, dear," Mrs. Drimley remarked when the glimmer in the trees disappeared, making room for a face. She slid her glasses down onto her eyes, and as her vision cleared, she made out the image of Mr. Appleton, who did, in fact, look insane. He looked over his shoulder, his features screwed up tightly with themselves at frequent intervals and seemed relentlessly overcome by twitchy fits of movement. This created an image completely contrary to the stately power he attempted to exude in the market. Here, he looked like a scared, albeit menacing, little boy.

"He wants to observe us, I believe," Mrs. Drimley announced. "He is forming a plan."

"A plan for what, I wonder?" Mulligan was decidedly less calm about the lurking figure in the wood than Mrs. Drimley seemed to be.

"Our demise, of course," Mrs. Drimley replied matter-of-factly.

"Oh, only our demise, then. I thought it would be something serious," Mulligan sarcastically retorted.

"Drama won't help us now, Mulligan. If it's a show he

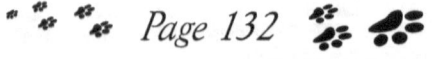

wants, we'll give him one. Hmmm..." Mulligan could just about see the gears turning in Mrs. Drimley's mind. She was cooking up an idea.

"We must keep our eyes on him, Mulligan. We mustn't let him go away without our knowing."

"What are we going to do? Sitting here isn't much of a show."

"No, it's not. I'll be going about my business as usual, Mulligan. There's nothing suspicious about a cat in the window all day, though, is there? You'll be my eyes today, Mulligan."

Mulligan considered this. Though the eyepiece did make him feel more stately, it did very little for his bad eye. He wore it anyway. It would take a great deal of concentration to keep his one good eye on the movements in the woods. What other choice did he really have? He would simply imagine to be a spy.

Through the Wood

It took all day. Mulligan's mind had imagined endless streams of schemes: Mr. Appleton was waiting for nightfall so he could come attack the house; Mr. Appleton was waiting for Mrs. Drimley to go outside where he would ambush her (this was proven false when Mrs. Drimley ventured outdoors to hang the wash and reentered the house unscathed.)

It wasn't until about four o'clock in the afternoon that the figure, which had grown steadier, and the face, which had grown more serene, began to move itself back into the depths of the woods. Mulligan leaped to find Mrs. Drimley who was loudly singing in an upstairs bedroom where she was airing the beds and dusting the never used furniture. She'd been making the most terrible racket all day long. Not a moment had passed without some shrill singing, whistling, or some banging of pots and pans. She'd made a big show of calling for Mulligan in all the usual cat-calling ways at one point, and carried on for so

long that Mulligan had been tempted to break his spy persona to tell her to kindly shut her yap.

Now, Mulligan was bounding up the stairs, taking two at a time. He slid around the corner to the hall and veered right midway down the hallway. "He's left."

"Yes, I can still see his head bobbing. Did you know there was a path in the woods, Mulligan? I've never seen it before, but now, standing here, I see it plain as day." Mrs. Drimley wondered again at her lack of knowledge of her surroundings.

"I don't venture into the woods much, on account of the prickly burrs, you know," Mulligan replied.

"He's gone far enough now, Mulligan. Let's go."

Mrs. Drimley scooped Mulligan into her arms, something he'd normally never allowed her to do, as they made their way through the brush toward the path. Branches and such had been freshly cleared, and young grass grew in patches. Underneath, though, there had evidently been a path once well worn. Mrs. Drimley stepped gingerly along the path, moving quickly and quietly. Every thirty seconds or so she stopped to listen. Mr. Appleton was not nearly so careful and was walking in a loud, clumsy manner, making him easy to both follow and avoid.

The woods were thick for a time, but soon, more light began to shine and there were pockets through which clearings could be seen. Mrs. Drimley slowed down when she heard voices. She moved off the path to her left and crouched low to the earth.

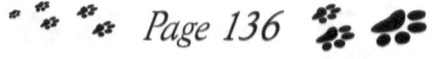

"Mulligan. Do you think you could climb a tree for a better look?" Mrs. Drimley prompted.

Mulligan sighed, then summoned his cat instincts to himself. "Here," he said, "take my vest. No, leave the eyepiece, I may need it."

Mrs. Drimley tucked the small vest into her apron pocket and watched as Mulligan dug his claws into tree bark. He didn't get far, though, before he slid noisily back down the tree, causing Mr. Appleton to peer frantically into the woods. "Quieter, Mulligan, you must be quieter. Here. Try this tree. You can leap up from branch to branch. Like climbing the cliff."

This worked much better, and Mulligan was soon so high Mrs. Drimley could not see him through the branches. She drew her attention to Mr. Appleton who seemed to be bragging. She could not hear well, so she crawled closer, thanking herself, once again, for her good sense in wearing her husband's pants. Once she could make out the words, she curled up next to a tree to watch and listen.

The house she was looking at, she assumed it was the Appleton's, was large, but unkempt. Not surprising, really, since the only well-groomed person in the whole lot was Mr. Appleton. She'd thought she'd heard a conversation but now she could tell that the only person speaking was Mr. Appleton, changing his inflection as though he were having a conversation, but leaving no room for any interjections from the others in the yard, his wife and children.

"I'll take care of her, though. Yes, tonight. Might as well get it over with. Gruesome task, though as long as she goes down with the house, it should be fairly simple. What else is to be done? She could upset the balance of this whole town, and I cannot have that. Mother would have been behind it, that's for sure. She would have sent me off with a..." At this Mr. Appleton pulled a soiled handkerchief from his pocket and dabbed his eyes. Mrs. Appleton, Mrs. Drimley noticed, had gone severely pale, and was so still you could almost mistake her for dead. A determined stiffness stifled her middle, and she drew in a sharp breath as though she were taking a risk even by breathing in his presence.

"You've never killed before." The words came out crackled, but with such force that they rang across the meadow. The children stopped and stared at their mother. It was obviously rare for her to speak this way.

Within seconds, she was flying backward and onto the ground from the force of the back of his left hand. He took the strides to stand over her carefully, then said through gritted teeth, "I will do what I have to do," and stalked toward the house, turning to add, "for my family, of course," with a hollow expression on his mottled face. Mrs. Drimley was now gripping the tree with such force that the bark was leaving an imprint on her cheek. Mrs. Appleton raised herself first onto her elbows, then up to her knees. It was then that Mulligan leapt with graceless

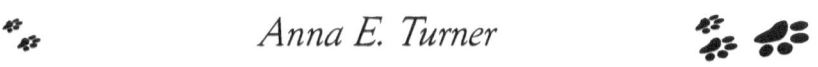

form through the leaves toward the ground where Mrs. Drimley clung to the tree. Mrs. Appleton's gaze turned sharply toward the sound in the wood, and the sisters eyes met. Tears flew down Mrs. Drimley's face and she moved to go toward her sister; to take her away. Again, though, fury filled her sister's eyes and that quick shake of her head forbade Mrs. Drimley to come forward. A sharp nod told Mrs. Drimley to go. And she did. Silently, Mulligan following closely behind her.

Mrs. Appleton Realizes

Mr. Appleton's mind was made up. As he'd sat all day in the blasted woods, a steady calm had grown in him. His mother had been wrong. He felt the guilt of disobeying her come in severe pangs shooting out from his heart, through his arms. She'd understand, he reassured himself. You have to do what you have to do, and hadn't he just spent the day in the woods, no shadow to be seen? She'd simply been mistaken. He felt moments of rage sitting there, thinking about the years of fear she'd cursed him with, but then would come another wave of guilt. He'd convinced himself over and over all through the day that she'd made an honest mistake; she'd been overcome by a silly fear that she'd passed on to him. No matter. He was free of it now.

He gathered the supplies he'd need to carry through the woods, and he made a torch to light before setting out on the path tonight. He'd stacked what he'd need—gasoline, matches, and the torch—at the entrance to the path. Just before dusk, he saw one of the children meddling with

the items. He bounded toward the child furiously. Would they never learn to respect his things?

Mrs. Appleton had sat silently at the kitchen table. She'd snuck into the house once Mr. Appleton had gone out rummaging around the shed. The kids ran raucously around the house, around her. She never moved, except to bring her coffee mug to her lips. Her cheek and head were throbbing, but that had become a constant in her life since she'd followed Mr. Appleton away from her father's home. Father, so useless in that chair in that stinking shack. She'd thought a man of action would be superior. Certainly Mr. Appleton appeared superior, but she knew she was doomed the moment she met his mother. By then, of course, it had been too late. She'd instantly understood the arrangement that had been made at her expense. She'd been a fool. She'd known that immediately, too.

Mrs. Appleton took a long sip of tepid coffee, her eyes glazed so that the children running by were blurs, her ears ringing so loudly the baby's cries seemed to come from a faraway land.

He'd never killed anyone. The moment she understood his plans, she had another of her instant realizations. He could kill. The thought almost made her laugh. It almost made her giddy. In fact, laughter rang in her mind as she sat there silently, unmoving. Then the truth clutched her around the sternum, summoning her away from her haze.

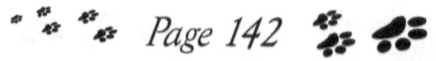

Mrs. Appleton blinked away the fog in her eyes. She awoke so forcefully that for a moment she could feel and see and hear what she had closed herself to over years and years of sinking deeper into her despairing self. Her head darted up at the sound of a grunt and looked up from the table out the door to see Mr. Appleton race toward her small child, lift him off the ground and throw him.

These things had happened before; of course they had. But Mrs. Appleton had stifled all her senses so she could not really feel. At that moment, the brief parting of the fog left room for her to see, hear, feel it all: her child flying across the yard, his whimpers, the way he curled up on the ground, coiling himself almost into nothing. All the dampening layers fell away. She grabbed the skillet off the stove. And she ran.

Mr. Appleton was reaching down to haul the boy up and teach him a lesson he wouldn't forget when the blow came on the back of his head. He fell instantly. Mrs. Appleton cautiously leaned over him. He was still breathing, but he didn't respond when she kicked him.

She gathered the small boy in her arms and summoned her older children, telling them to gather all the others They were to wait for her on the path in the woods. Then she grabbed Mr. Appleton by the ankles and drug him over the rough yard, through the back door, and left him in the hallway.

He still wasn't stirring. She ran to the pile he'd left by the path and grabbed the gas can. She didn't think, she

just moved. She ran around the perimeter of the house, dousing the frame with gas. When she got back to the door where she'd began, she nervously retrieved a match from the box. She knelt, hands trembling, frozen for several minutes. She thought she heard a groan.

She couldn't do it. She could not light the match. Frustrated tears streaming down her face, she ran, carrying the gas can to the pile her husband had made, and ran into the woods to find her family.

The Potency

Mrs. Drimley and Mulligan ran out of the woods, breathless. She looked down at him, both of their eyes silently imploring, "What are we going to do?" Then they both spoke at once.

"First we must..."

"I think we should..."

"...block the path..."

"...find help to stop..."

"...you'll keep watch..."

The trouble was they couldn't understand a word the other was saying. They were panicking.

"STOP!" Mrs. Drimley shouted. "We must calm down. Now." Then she took a steadying breath.

"Yes, be calm while the man plots how he's going to kill us!" Mulligan exclaimed incredulously.

"It is the only way to stop him," Mrs. Drimley replied matter-of-factly. "What are our strengths, Mulligan? What do we know of his weaknesses? Who do we know who can help?"

 *The Cat at Mrs. Drimley's Door*

Mrs. Drimley and Mulligan stayed in this state of brainstorming for some time. They warily eyed the path, and were as skittish as they'd ever been in their lives, but they managed to remain focused. Until, that is, they heard the sound of a spoon clanking on a pot in the kitchen, and the unmistakable hum that goes along with cooking. Together, the two crawled to the nearby kitchen window which was still standing open from its earlier airing.

"Come on in, you two," a voice shouted merrily, "Can't save your lives on an empty stomach."

"Florie," Mrs. Drimley whispered to Mulligan, who in spite of his deep longing to roll his eyes, was relieved to have a third party on the defense team.

The two walked around the house to the kitchen door and gaped at the site in the kitchen. There on the stove was an enormous pot. Florie saw them eyeing it. "I brought my own, in case you didn't have one large enough," she said with a grin.

"But how did you get it here?" Mrs. Drimley questioned, aghast.

"It was no trouble," Florie replied, still grinning. "I found your salt, Elsa, horribly low, you'll need to order some."

"Why are you making such a large pot, Florie?" Mrs. Drimley asked.

"You're having company."

"Oh yes, feed the murderous wretch. Let's do!" Mulligan mocked.

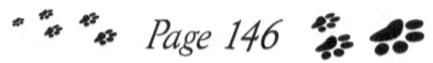 *Page 146*

Florie laughed hoarsely, "Oh, not him, dear. Not him."

"Florie, night is about to fall. Mr. Appleton, he's coming, Florie. We heard him. He's been watching us. He wants to kill me. He's coming tonight. We've got to find a way to stop him."

"And so you shall, but first, you have time to eat. He won't be up to coming just now," Florie replied with a twinkle in her eye. She was putting on a good show of confidence, but Mrs. Drimley could tell she was concerned.

"What do you know?" Mrs. Drimley demanded.

"I only know what I must, and I can only do what I can," she said with real sympathy. Then she took a taste of the soup she was cooking, "Wooo-weeee! Now that is potent!"

"I'm so looking forward to eating it now," Mulligan replied saucily.

Florie laughed again, "How surly you are as a cat, dear!"

Mulligan merely rolled his eyes, thinking the old lady must be out of her mind.

"What can you tell me, Florie? I need help," Mrs. Drimley implored.

Florie was ladling up the soup when the knock came at the door. Mrs. Drimley and Mulligan both froze, but Florie calmly said, "Well, answer it, dear."

Mrs. Drimley sat shuddering for a few seconds more, then resolutely found her feet and made them move toward the door. "Who is it?" she called, silently rebuking her voice for shaking.

"It's me. Angeline. I have the children. Please. Let us in."

Mrs. Drimley paused, holding her breath. She'd seen that her sister could be vindictive, cruel to her children. This could be a set up. But that pull in her bones was there.

"You're not safe, Elsa," Mrs. Appleton continued urgently through the door.

Mrs. Drimley glanced at Florie and Mulligan who both nodded. She gave the door knob a solid turn and opened it quickly, as if to get it over with. Though she was afraid of what she might see on the other side of the door, all that was there was her sister, tears streaming down her stoic face, and her brood of filthy, blank faced children.

"Who's hungry?" Florie asked, bustling over toward the door with a tray of bowls. "Come in and fill your bellies, little ones!" Florie pounced on the children as though she'd been waiting a century for the chance to feed them. "Yes, come in," Mrs. Drimley added, though her voice was dry and strained.

The children shoved into the sitting room where Florie seated them around and sat them up with bowls, with stacks of books and trays for tables. Then she returned to the kitchen where few words had passed, and dished up four more bowls.

"Eat up," she said resolutely.

Mrs. Drimley and Mrs. Appleton methodically plunged spoons into bowls and into mouths, each of them lost.

Mulligan's lapping made soft sounds while the women's spoons scraped the sides and bottoms of their bowls.

Mrs. Drimley agreed with Florie's assessment. The soup was, indeed, potent, so potent it returned them to themselves, delivering them from their panic. Mrs. Appleton calmly explained what she had done, and what she could not do. Mrs. Drimley declared her disinclination to allow Mr. Appleton to have his way under any circumstances. Mulligan pledged his assistance. And Florie floated between adults and children, assuring everyone that everything was just as it should be. A plan slowly developed which they all agreed should at least buy them a little more time.

After bellies were full, Mrs. Drimley led the children and Mrs. Appleton up to the bedrooms that had never been used, and Florie stayed to tuck each one in. Then Mrs. Appleton took her post in the east facing window of the third floor. Mulligan had set off to be a lookout in the woods.

Mrs. Drimley stood guard at the opening of the path, determined, whatever else, that they all be in one piece when morning came.

Through the Fog and Shadows

The back of Mr. Appleton's head was throbbing in tandem with his heartbeat. It took some time to realize that he was awake, that he was on the floor in the hallway, that all was silent and darkness had fallen. What day was it? What had happened? Where was his family? He deftly moved his fingers and felt alertness seep into his mind like hot water into a tea bag. The more alert he grew, the more aware he was of the pain.

He reached his hand back to feel his head and met a sizeable lump that stung when he touched it. A crusty layer of dried blood covered the center of the lump and he flinched as his fingers tore a small flake from the scab. Mr. Appleton put his hands beneath him and raised his shoulders from the ground, then felt the world spin around him. Shutting his eyes, he gathered himself and brought his knees to the floor beneath him. He gripped the wall as he pulled himself upright, leaning heavily on it as he walked toward the door.

He tried to shout for his miserable wife, but the attempt to speak made the pain in his skull surge so forcefully he winced and drew his head into his hands. He made his way to the wooden stoop below the door and sat himself gingerly upon it, letting his eyes adjust. Still with his head in his hands, he surveyed the yard. When his eyes fell on the gas can, the day came back to him. The awareness that he needed to get on with his plan gave him a surge of energy that propelled him across the yard, stumbling, tripping to his knees once, then scrambling back up. Again he fell to his knees when he reached the torch, matches, and gas can; this time on purpose. It took several attempts to light the torch.

He wasted many matches, but eventually he had a decent fire going. He'd done this before, he reminded himself. Nothing to it. No matter that the lady was inside this time. That was not his problem.

He was still dizzy, disoriented. He knew he would have to walk carefully, slowly. No sense in burning the whole forest down.

He'd made it halfway when he saw it. At first he thought his eyes were tricking him, but no, there was light shining back at him. Flickering first here then there. And the leaves were rustling as though something was moving through them.

"Who's there?" his voice sounded gruff, but weak. "I said, who's there."

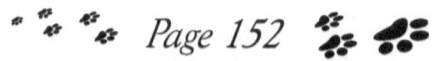

He turned abruptly at a sound behind him, but there was no light, no movement. Walking backward, he continued through the woods, but as he turned, there it was again. A flicker of light.

Mulligan had caught on almost immediately to what was happening. It was his eyepiece! It was reflecting firelight! Well, he could have fun with this. He leapt from tree to tree turning his head this way and that to catch the light. He could not get too far away, but being too close would not work either. Slowly, slowly, Mulligan toyed with his prey. Just like a mouse, Mulligan thought condescendingly.

Mr. Appleton swung the torch around recklessly, looking for whatever was beaming light at him. He could not continue to yell. The throbbing in his head was nearly unbearable. He looked up and around wildly, peering in every direction with each step.

Then he saw it. A shadow leaping from tree top to tree top. He dropped to his knees for the third time that night, this time in utter panic. Shakily, he forced himself up. He had to get through the woods.

He steeled his gaze forward, shuddering with each leap of the shadow. It was behind him now; it was following him. He could hear it close on his heels. Any minute now, he could be history.

His head throbbed. His heart pounded. The only thing that propelled him forward was the thought of being ousted from his seat of control by the Drimley woman. He had to go on.

"Get me through this, mother," he pleaded, "Get me through this and I won't be foolish enough to enter the woods again." Finally he saw light coming from a window through the trees. There, he was almost there. In the window, a woman sat motionless. It looked as though she were asleep. This would be too easy. He rushed ahead into the yard and nearly collapsed yet again, this time from the fright of coming face to face with the very woman he thought he'd seen sleeping in the window. He looked up at the window, but it was empty.

Mrs. Drimley stood before him calmly. "I've been waiting for you," she said with a smile, "You'll go no further, tonight, I'm afraid."

What Fear Did

"It's time to go home, Mr. Appleton," Mrs. Drimley said with a too sweet, knowing smile.

Mr. Appleton dropped the gas can and attempted to rush forward toward Mrs. Drimley. He was clumsy, though, and she merely stepped aside to avoid him.

"You'll not want to do that, Mr. Appleton. For what you fear most is my very good friend. He takes threats against me quite seriously, and I'm afraid he's had just about enough of you. It's time to go home, Mr. Appleton." She stated slowly. "Through the wood, you know."

"I'll not go b-b-b-back there," Mr. Appleton stammered as he held his hand in his head, "Not until I've done what I came to do."

"Oh, you'll not be doing what you came to do at all, Mr. Appleton," Mrs. Drimley replied calmly, "Will he, Shadow?"

"No, he won't," Mulligan's voice boomed into the clearing so loudly that even Mrs. Drimley had to suppress a shudder. However had Florie managed that, she wondered.

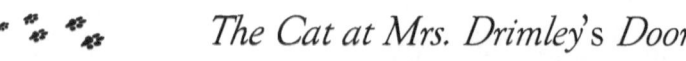 

And then the shadow began to grow into the yard from the woods, another contribution from Florie, obviously. It crept slowly toward Mr. Appleton, nearly oozing its way out of the woods around Mr. Appleton, forcing him back toward the path. Mr. Appleton wildly swung his torch around, but the firelight couldn't touch the darkness of this shadow.

"You're only chance," Mulligan's voice boomed, "is to out run me."

He's enjoying this a little too much, Mrs. Drimley thought to herself as Mr. Appleton tripped over himself back to the woods. She watched his light until it disappeared, growing steadily smaller. She was confident that Mulligan would see to it that he stay out of the woods and off of the path at least for this night. Still, she sat, keeping watch and waiting for Mulligan's return.

On the other side of the woods, Mr. Appleton had just raced into the clearing. He ran toward his house, crying for his mother to save him.

"Open the door, mother! Open the door."

His head throbbed. His heart was in his throat. His feet pounded the earth below him, and the pain each step shot through his brain was unbearable. Almost there, he thought. He spared a glance back, sure he saw the shadow taunting him from the woods, but not leaving it! He'd made it! He turned, and slowed to a backward jog.

"Ha! I beat you! Did you see, Mother? I beat the shadow. I beat it, Mother. Now we'll never have to..." But he never finished his sentence for he tripped on the wooden stoop he'd sat on just an hour before, fell back sharply onto his already wounded head, dropping the torch on the way down onto gas soaked grass that hungrily lapped up the flames. The flames fed themselves mercilessly on the house and the unconscious Mr. Appleton.

Mulligan had stopped midway through the wood to groom himself, sure that Mr. Appleton would see his own way home. Now he sat waiting on a tree branch, just to be sure the foul man didn't recover his courage and make another attempt to come through the wood.

So it was that Mulligan was the first to see the flickering flames. He crept cautiously forward through the trees. By the time he reached the clearing, the house was ablaze.

Florie soon appeared by his side. She had the contract gripped in her hand.

"This is not what we'd intended," Mulligan said, though now he was less Mulligan than before. When his task was complete, he always remembered it all.

"No, it never works like we intend. But this is exactly what fear does. A troubled ending this time, dear. But think of the ladies. And the townspeople. They have a brand new chance."

The silence flowed between them as they watched the

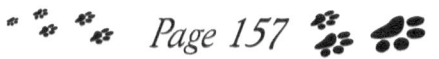

house burn, knowing that Mr. Appleton was far beyond their help. Florie laid her hand on the paw of her old friend and said sympathetically, "Ours isn't an easy path, is it?"

"Certainly not."

"It's goodbye now, you know. We'll be moving on. Our task is done. I've left notes, as it's usually the best way. It never is easy," Florie said slowly, watching her longtime companion intently. This was always the hardest part for him.

"No, never easy. I quite liked being Mulligan. And that Mrs. Drimley...I would like to see how she does. It's not fair, Florie. I never think of the goodbyes when I begin these things, you know. I wish you would remind me."

"Oh, Edgar. But how could you begin if you only thought of the endings? And where would Mrs. Drimley be without her Mulligan?"

"Yes, where would she be? I suppose I have to go on, then, to the next round of things?"

"I'm afraid we always have to do that, my dear."

"Very well, then."

And just like that, they were gone.

Epilogue

Mrs. Drimley looked up from her seat at the lately enlarged table. She'd hired a man from town to come out and build a table large enough for the whole family. Then she had set it on top of the rug she had made with Mr. Drimley's old shirts. She peered over the windowsill to count the running heads in the yard, a habit she had developed to still her watchful heart.

Her sister was out hanging the sheets, which she'd stripped from the beds that morning. The youngest Appleton sat on top of the damp heap as though it were a throne and shook her little rattle like a queen's scepter. She'd never know, thought Mrs. Drimley. She would never know what it was to be kicked aside, to be only a marginally useful nuisance.

Mrs. Drimley reached into her apron pocket and fingered Mulligan's vest, which she had kept near her since that night. She wished she'd known then that he was going, but what difference would it have made? Goodbye

would have been far too painful. She could hardly believe only a year had passed since Mr. Drimley had left and Mulligan arrived, since the satisfying mundane had been turned on its head, and she with it. Her heart still ached for both of them.

Mulligan had never come back, but there had been a note from Florie that explained things, supposedly. Who could believe what was written in that letter? But then, who could believe any of the events that had passed over the course of the year? Had any of it been real? Mrs. Drimley feared she may have lost her mind.

Everything had changed the day she stopped carrying the firewood, boiling the water, stripping the beds, airing the house, and dropping fish heads, one by one, into the stew. Mrs. Drimley wondered now why they had lived on such a meager portion. Her stomach, so full of morning pancakes and syrup, could not make sense of it. Her bones only knew it had been her doing. Her choice. Just as it had been her choice to go on living when the world she'd known those twenty-seven years with Mr. Drimley were simply and suddenly over.

Mrs. Drimley stood at the window, her memory overwhelming her senses. The fade to black. The sorrow. The pain and determined resurrection. The unexpected upheaval of entering the world outside her door. Life seemed to be everything but gentle. Mrs. Drimley knew on that morning more than she'd ever known before,

more than she'd ever know after, about what it took to stay alive.

It took going on breathing. It took constant choosing, but only one choice at a time, each decision dependent on ...stitching. And counting heads, even when the only head you have to count is your own.

And, maybe, a talking cat's.